One Doze

One Dozen Stories

SATYAJIT RAY

Translated from the Bengali by Satyajit Ray and
Gopa Majumdar

Introduction by Chitra Banerjee Divakaruni

PUFFIN

PUFFIN BOOKS

Published by the Penguin Group

Penguin Books India Pvt. Ltd, 11 Community Centre, Panchsheel Park, New Delhi 110 017, India

Penguin Group (USA) Inc., 375 Hudson Street, New York, New York 10014, USA

Penguin Group (Canada), 90 Eglinton Avenue East, Suite 700, Toronto, Ontario, M4P 2Y3, Canada (a division of Pearson Penguin Canada Inc.)

Penguin Books Ltd, 80 Strand, London WC2R 0RL, England

Penguin Ireland, 25 St Stephen's Green, Dublin 2, Ireland (a division of Penguin Books Ltd)

Penguin Group (Australia), 250 Camberwell Road, Camberwell, Victoria 3124, Australia (a division of Pearson Australia Group Pty Ltd)

Penguin Group (NZ), 67 Apollo Drive, Rosedale, North Shore 0632, New Zealand (a division of Pearson New Zealand Ltd)

Penguin Group (South Africa) (Pty) Ltd, 24 Sturdee Avenue, Rosebank, Johannesburg 2196, South Africa

Penguin Books Ltd, Registered Offices: 80 Strand, London WC2R 0RL, England

First published in Puffin by Penguin Books India 2008

Text copyright © The Estate of Satyajit Ray 2008

This anthology and translation copyright © Penguin Books India 2008

The stories in this book were first published in Bengali as *Ek Dojon Goppo* by Ananda Publishers Pvt. Ltd 1970

A version of 'Bipin Chowdhury's Lapse of Memory' first appeared in *Target* in 1984; Gopa Majumdar's translation of 'The Two Magicians' first appeared in *Namaste* in 1989; versions of 'Patol Babu, Film Star' and 'Indigo' appeared in *Stories* by Satyajit Ray published by Secker and Warburg 1987.

All rights reserved

10 9 8 7 6 5 4 3 2 1

ISBN 9780143330912

Typeset in Minion by Mantra Virtual Services, New Delhi

Printed at DeUnique Printers, New Delhi

Contents

Introduction

Some books take us back to the magical days of our childhood, recreating for us the time when we awoke in the morning to a certain light in the sky that suggested an adventure might be waiting around the corner. At night, when we listened to the tales told by our grandparents, shadows thrown against the wall took on the shapes of terrifying, fascinating beasts. Who knew where a ghost might be lurking, or a man-eating plant, or a monster who had taken on the shape of a mathematics teacher? Who knew when, during a mundane evening stroll, one might get the chance to step into a time machine?

Satyajit Ray's *One Dozen Stories* is such a book, a collection of stories that are, happily for new readers, published here for the first time in English translation in a single volume.

The other day I sat down on my living room couch with *One Dozen Stories*, planning to sample only one or two, because I had other work that needed to be done. To my surprise, before I knew it, I was curled up in bed under a quilt, devouring the book, quite unable to stop. Reading, I was struck by how well Ray knew children and what delighted them. Perhaps a part of him had remained a child always, the part that created delightful magical adventure films like *Goopy Gyne Bagha Byne* and *Sonar Kella*.

The stories in this book pull you in right away, opening up for you the mysterious world that adults have sometimes grown too cynical to believe in. (Perhaps that is the reason why mystery and magic elude them.) Ray's universe is filled with charming, eccentric characters who are interested in the strange and esoteric—Kanti Babu, who has dedicated his life to the study of carnivorous plants, Anath Babu, who travels from one end of India to the other in search of authentic ghosts, or Aniruddha Bose, who ends up spending a night in a deserted bungalow belonging to an indigo planter—a night which changes his life! Some of Ray's characters are quixotic and unworldly, and for them we feel a protective affection: Badan Babu, who wants more than anything to find the perfect story to tell his young son—and whose wish comes true in an unexpected way, or Patol Babu, the impoverished actor who chooses the satisfaction of the perfect performance over making money, or my favourite, the meek Banku Babu, who is mercilessly teased by his friends until an amazing experience gives him the confidence to turn the tables on them. These characters are not successful in the usual sense of the word. They are sometimes bullied or tricked by more worldly-wise people, or even taken advantage of, but the reader is left feeling that perhaps in the game of life, they are the true victors.

And then, of course, there is the inimitable Feluda, who

appears in two of the stories: our very own Bengali Sherlock Holmes, aided by his young cousin Tapesh. Feluda is probably Satyajit Ray's most popular literary hero—intrepid, intelligent, insouciant—but not above playing a trick or two on his cousin. He will delight young readers—and the young at heart—as he unravels mysteries, saves the endangered and exposes villains with elan.

The city of Calcutta is also a character in these stories—Calcutta and a whole Bengali way of life—drinking tea, eating jalebies, pushing one's way into buses crowded beyond belief, climbing the rooftops of ancient, crumbling buildings to keep an eye on the activities of neighbours, leisurely reading the Bengali paper on a weekend morning while drinking more tea, and engaging in that favourite activity of Bengalis: adda—a heated discussion of world issues, or the telling of tall tales.

From time to time, Ray's characters leave their beloved, and sometimes infuriating, city for the Bengal countryside, into which they make excursions in search of adventure. This countryside is filled with trees: shirish, peepal, bamboo and tamarind; it is green with rice fields and brimming with lakes. Here and there one finds old dak bungalows, once owned by the British, or perhaps a ruined temple or river ghat with its worn stone steps. As I read the stories, I was transported into this landscape, and through it, into an earlier, more magical time.

One Dozen Stories is not merely an entertaining read.

There are lessons here for both adults and children, but they are lightly handled, cloaked in humour, a zest for life and a charming narrative innocence. Reader: I don't want to colour your vision by telling you what I learned. I invite you to make your own discoveries. An adventure awaits you, and I will not keep you from it any longer. Remember only this: approach the stories with what the poet Samuel Taylor Coleridge, another lover of the mysterious, asked of his readers—a willing suspension of disbelief.

August 2008   Chitra Banerjee Divakaruni

The Hungry Septopus

There it was again—the sound of someone rattling the knocker on my front door. I gave an involuntary exclamation of annoyance. This was the fourth interruption this evening. How was a man expected to work? There was no sign of Kartik, either. He had left for the market a long time ago.

I was forced to leave my desk and open the door myself. It took me a while to recognize the man who was standing outside. When I did, I felt profoundly startled. Why, it was Kanti Babu!

'What a surprise! Do come in,' I said.

'So you have recognized me?'

'Yes, but it wasn't easy.'

I showed him into the living room and offered him a seat. I had not seen him in ten years. His appearance had undergone a remarkable change in that time. In 1950, I had seen the same man in a forest in Assam, jumping around with a magnifying glass in his hand. He was nearly fifty then, but all his hair was still black. He bubbled all the time with energy and endless enthusiasm. Such vitality would be hard to find even among the young.

'Are you still interested in orchids?' Kanti Babu asked.

There was an orchid in a pot resting on my window sill. It was, in fact, a gift from Kanti Babu himself. I wasn't really interested in plants any more. It was Kanti Babu who had once aroused my curiosity about them. But after he went abroad, I had lost my interest gradually. There were other hobbies and interests, too, but I had given them up as well. Now my only passion was writing.

Things had changed over the years. Now it was possible to make money just by writing. To tell the truth, my last three books had brought me an income that was almost wholly sufficient to meet my household expenses. Not that I had a big house to run—there was only my widowed mother to take care of, and my servant, Kartik. I still had a job, but was hoping to give it up if my writing continued to bring me success. I would write full-time, and when I could take a break, I would travel. That was my plan.

Suddenly, Kanti Babu shivered. 'Are you feeling cold? Shall I close the window? The winter in Calcutta this year . . .' I began.

'No, no. You saw me shiver? It happens sometimes. I am getting old, you see. So my nerves are no longer . . .'

I wanted to ask a lot of questions. Kartik had returned. I asked him to bring us tea.

'I won't take up a lot of your time,' said Kanti Babu. 'I came across one of your novels recently. So I got in touch with your publisher, took your address, and well, here I am. There is a special reason why I had to see you.'

'Yes? Tell me all about it. But before you do, there's so much I want to know. When did you return? Where were you all these years? Where are you now?'

'I returned two years ago. Before that I was in America. Now I live in Barasat.'

'Barasat?'

'I bought a house there.'

'Does it have a garden?'

'Yes.'

'And a greenhouse?'

In the house that I had visited before, Kanti Babu had a lovely greenhouse, in which he tended, with great care, several of his rare plants. I had seen such a large number of strange and weird plants there! Of orchids alone he had more than sixty varieties. One could easily pass a whole day just looking at and enjoying their different colours and other characteristics.

Kanti Babu paused for a second before saying, 'Yes, there is a greenhouse.'

'So you're still as mad about plants as you were ten years ago?'

'Yes.'

Kanti Babu was staring at the opposite wall. Automatically, I followed his gaze. The wall was covered by the skin of a Royal Bengal tiger, including the head.

'Does it seem familiar to you?' I asked.

'Is it that same tiger?'

'Yes. See that hole close to its left ear? That's where the bullet passed through.'

'You were a remarkable shot. Can you still shoot with such perfect accuracy?'

'I don't know. I haven't used my gun for a long time. I gave up shikar more than five years ago.'

'Why?'

'I had had enough. I mean, I had killed enough animals. After all, I'm not getting any younger. It was time to stop destroying wildlife.'

'Really? So have you stopped eating meat? Are you now a vegetarian?'

'No. No, I am not.'

'Why not? Killing a wild animal is just plain killing. Say you destroy a tiger, or a crocodile, or a bison, and then you hang its head, or just its horns on your wall. What happens? Your room acquires a special air, some of your visitors are horrified, others are impressed, and you can relive the moments of your youthful adventures. That's all. But think of the chicken, goats and fish you are not just killing, but also eating every day. It's more than mere destruction, isn't it? Why, it's the digestion of a living creature!'

There was really nothing I could say in reply. So I remained silent.

Kartik brought us tea.

Kanti Babu remained lost in thought for a few moments, then suddenly shivered again and picked up his cup. 'It isn't unusual for one particular animal to eat another. Nature made things that way. See that gecko lying in wait over there?' he asked.

Over a calendar on the wall sprawled a gecko, staring unblinkingly at an insect, just a couple of inches away from its mouth. Then it moved slowly, ever so slowly, before springing forward in one leap and swallowing its prey.

'There!' exclaimed Kanti Babu. 'That takes care of his dinner. Eating is all most creatures are concerned with. Just think about it. A tiger would eat a man, a man would eat a goat, and a goat would eat anything! Doesn't it all seem terribly wild, primitive and violent? Yet, that is how nature wills it. Stop this cycle, and the whole natural order would be thrown out of gear.'

'Perhaps being a vegetarian is more . . . er . . . civilized?'

'Who told you that? You think leaves and vegetables and plants are lifeless? Do they not live?'

'Yes, of course they do. Thanks to Jagadish Bose and you, I can never forget about the life of plants. But it's different, isn't it? I mean, animals and plants are not the same, surely?'

'Oh? You think there are a lot of differences between the two?'

'Aren't there? A tree cannot move, walk, make a noise, express thoughts or feelings—in fact, there's no way to find out if a tree has a mind at all. Isn't that true?'

Kanti Babu opened his mouth to speak, then shut it without saying a word. Silently, he finished his tea and sat with his head bowed. Eventually, when he looked up and met my eyes, I suddenly felt afraid to see the look of tragic uncertainty in his. Truly, the change in the man was extraordinary.

When he spoke, his voice was quiet. 'Parimal,' he said, 'I live twenty-one miles away. And I am fifty-eight years old. But despite my age and the long distance I had to travel, I took the trouble to get your address and visit you here. Surely I don't need to tell you now that there is a very important reason behind my visit? You can see that, can't you? Or have you lost all your intelligence in trying to produce popular fiction? Are you looking at me right now and thinking: here's a new type—I can use him in a story?'

I had to look away, flushing with embarrassment. Kanti Babu was right. The thought of using him as a character had indeed occurred to me.

'Remember this,' he went on. 'If you lose touch with the realities of life, whatever you write will simply be lies, empty and hollow. Besides, no matter how lively your imagination is, what emerges from it can never match the surprises real life can come up with. Anyway, I didn't come here to give you a lecture. I came, to tell you the truth, to ask a favour.'

Kanti Babu glanced at the tiger again. What favour was he talking about?

'Do you still have your gun, or did you get rid of it?'

I gave a slight start, and glanced quickly at him. Why did he mention my gun?

'No, I have still got it. But it may well be rusted. Why do you ask?'

'Can you come to my house tomorrow, with your gun?'

I scanned his face. No, there was not even the slightest sign to imply that he might be joking.

'Of course,' he added, 'you'll need bullets, too. The gun alone won't be good enough.'

I could not immediately think of anything to say in reply to Kanti Babu's request. It even occurred to me once that perhaps he had gone mad, although one could not be sure. He was certainly given to crazy whims. Or else why should he have risked his life in a jungle to look for rare plants?

'I can quite easily take my gun, there's no problem,' I said finally. 'But I am dying to know the reason why it might be needed. Is there an animal bothering the residents in your area? Or perhaps there are burglars and thieves?'

'I will explain everything once you get there. Who knows, we might not even have to use the gun. But even if we do, I can assure you that you will not be arrested!'

Kanti Babu rose to his feet. Then he came closer and laid a hand on my shoulder. 'I came to you because when I last saw you, you had struck me as a man who would welcome a new experience, very much like myself. Besides, I don't know many other people. The number of people I actually visited was always small, and now I see virtually no one. The handful of people I could think of contacting are all very different, you see. None of them has the special qualities that you have.'

Just for a minute, I could feel, in the sudden tightening of my muscles, the same thrill that the mere mention of an adventure used to bring, all those years ago.

'When would you like me to get there? How would I find your house?' I asked.

'I'll tell you. Just go straight down Jessore Road until you get to the railway station in Barasat. Then you need to find a lake called Madhumurali Deeghi. It's another four miles from the station. Anyone there will tell you where it is. Next to the lake is an old and abandoned indigo factory. My house is right behind it. Do you have a car?'

'No, but a friend of mine has.'

'Who is this friend?'

'His name is Abhijit. He and I were in college together.'

'What kind of a man is he? Do I know him?'

'No, I don't think so. But he's a good man. I mean, if you're wondering whether he's reliable, I can tell you that he is. Totally.'

'Very well. You may bring him with you. But please make sure that you reach my house before evening. It's important, needless to say.'

Kanti Babu left. Since I did not have a telephone at home, I went to our local chemist just across the road to ring

Abhijit. 'Come to my house at once,' I said to him, 'I've got something urgent to discuss.'

'Urgent? You mean you've got a new story you'd like to read out to me? I'll go to sleep again, let me tell you!'

'No, no. It's not about a story. Something quite different.'

'What is it? Why are you speaking so softly?'

'I've come to know about a pup. Mastiff. The man selling it is sitting in my house, right now.'

I knew Abhijit would not stir out of his house unless I could lure him out by talking of dogs. He had eleven dogs. Each one of them belonged to a different species. Three of those dogs had won prizes. Even five years ago, things were different. But now, Abhijit thought and dreamt of nothing but dogs.

Apart from his love of dogs, there was something else that made him very special. Abhijit had unflinching faith in my talent and judgement. When my first novel was turned down by publishers, it was Abhijit who provided the money to publish it privately. 'Mind you,' he told me, 'I know nothing of books and literature. But if you have written this book, it cannot possibly be absolute garbage. These publishers are complete idiots!' As it happened, things turned out quite well. The book was well received and sold a large number of copies. As a result, Abhijit's faith in me grew stronger.

He turned up soon enough, and gave me a painful punch when he discovered that I had lied about the pup. However, seeing his enthusiasm regarding the real reason for calling him out, I soon forgot the pain.

'We haven't had an outing for long time, have we?' Abhijit said eagerly. 'The last time was when we went snipe-shooting in Shonarpur. But who is this man? What's it all about? Why don't you come clean, my friend?'

'How can I, when he told me nothing? Besides, a little mystery is a good thing. I like it. It should give us the chance to use our imagination.'

'All right, but who is this man? What does he do?'

'His name is Kanticharan Chatterjee. Does that mean anything to you? He was once a professor of botany. Used to teach in Scottish Church College. Then he gave up his job and began looking for rare plants in jungles and forests. Sometimes he wrote about them. He had a wonderful collection of plants, particularly of orchids.'

'How did you get to meet him?'

'I met him in a forest bungalow in Assam. I was there to hunt down a tiger. He was hunting everywhere for a nepenthes.'

'Hunting for what?'

'Nepenthes. It's the botanical name for what is commonly called a pitcher-plant. You can get it in the forests of Assam. It eats insects. I did not see it myself, but Kanti Babu told me about it.'

'Eats insects? A plant? It . . . chomps on insects?'

'You did not ever study botany, did you?'

'No.'

'I have seen pictures of this plant. There is no reason to sound so sceptical. It exists.'

'Okay. What happened next?'

'Very little. I finished my shikar and came away. Kanti Babu stayed on. I have no idea whether he found that plant or not. What I was afraid of was that he might be killed by a wild animal, or bitten by a snake. When he set off to look for a plant, he thought of nothing else, not even of the dangers in a forest. After coming back to Calcutta, I met him only a couple of times. But I thought of him often, because for a time I developed quite a passion for orchids. Kanti Babu offered to bring me some good quality orchids from America.'

'America? This man went to America?'

'Yes. One of his articles was published in an English botanical journal. It made him quite well known in those circles. Then he was invited to a conference of botanists in America. That was in 1951, or was it '52? That's when I last saw him.'

'Was he there all this while? What was he doing?'

'No idea. Hopefully, he'll tell us tomorrow.'

'He's not . . . ? I mean, is he perhaps a little eccentric?'

'Not any more than you. I can tell you that much. You fill your life with dogs. He fills his with plants.'

*

We were now going down Jessore Road in the direction of Barasat, travelling in Abhijit's Standard.

There was a third passenger in the car. It was Abhijit's dog, Badshah. It was my own fault, really. I should have known that, unless otherwise instructed, Abhijit was bound to bring one of his eleven dogs.

Badshah was a Rampur hound, a ferocious animal. He had spread himself out on the back seat and was sitting very comfortably as its sole occupant, looking out of the window at the wide, open rice fields. Each time a stray dog from a local village came into view, Badshah gave a mild, contemptuous growl.

When I saw Abhijit arrive with Badshah, I tried to put up a faint protest. At this, Abhijit said, 'I don't have a great deal of faith in your skill, you see. That's why I brought him along. You haven't handled your gun for years. Should there be trouble, Badshah would probably be of far more use than you. He has an extraordinary sense of smell and is quite, quite fearless.'

Kanti Babu's house was not difficult to find. By the time we got there, it was half past two. A driveway led to the house, which was built in the style of a bungalow. Behind the house was an open space. A huge old shirish tree stood where this space ended. By its side was a structure with a tin roof. It looked like a small factory. In front of the house was a garden, at the end of which a long area was covered by another tin roof. A number of shining glass cases stood there in a row.

Kanti Babu came out to greet us, then frowned slightly as he saw Badshah. 'Is he a trained dog?' he asked.

'He'll listen to everything I say,' Abhijit told him. 'But if there's an untrained dog in the vicinity, and Badshah sees him, well, I couldn't tell you what he might do then. Is there such a dog?'

'No. But for the moment, please tie your dog to one of the bars on that window.'

Abhijit gave me a sidelong glance, winked and did as he was told, like an obedient child. Badshah protested a couple of times, but did not seem to mind too much.

We sat on cane chairs on the front veranda. 'My servant Prayag injured his right hand. So I made tea for you and put it in a flask. Let me know when you'd like some.'

It was a very quiet and peaceful place. I could hear nothing but a few chirping birds. How could there be serious danger lurking somewhere in a place like this? I felt a little foolish, sitting with the gun in my hands. So I propped it up against a wall.

Abhijit could never sit still. He was very much a 'city' man; the beauties of nature offered by the countryside, the leaves on a peepal tree trembling in a slight breeze, or the call of an unknown bird, did nothing to move him. He looked around, shifted restlessly, and suddenly blurted out, 'Parimal told me that you once went to a forest in Assam looking for some weird plant, and nearly got gobbled up by a tiger. Is that true?'

This was something clse Abhijit was wont to do. He could not speak without exaggerating everything. I felt afraid Kanti Babu might be offended. But he just laughed and said, 'Do you always think of a tiger whenever you think of danger? But that's not surprising, many people would do that. No, I never came across a tiger. Leeches in the forest caused me some discomfort, but that was nothing serious, either.'

'Did you find that plant?'

The same question had occurred to me, too.

'Which plant?'

'Oh, that . . . pot? . . . No, pitcher plant or something?'

'Yes. Nepenthes. Yes, I did find it and, in fact, have still got it. I'll show it to you. I am no longer interested in ordinary plants; now I restrict myself only to carnivorous ones. I've got rid of most of my orchids, too.'

Kanti Babu rose and went indoors. Abhijit and I exchanged glances. Carnivorous plants? Plants that ate meat? A few pages and pictures I had studied fifteen years ago in a book on botany dimly wafted before my eyes.

When Kanti Babu re-emerged, there was a bottle in his hand. It contained house-crickets and a few other insects, still alive. The stopper on the bottle, I noticed, had tiny holes, like those on a pepper-shaker.

'Feeding time!' said Kanti Babu with a smile. 'Come with me.'

We followed Kanti Babu out to the long strip of ground at the back of his garden which contained the glass cases.

Each of the cases held a different plant. I had seen none of them before.

'Except for nepenthes,' Kanti Babu told us, 'not a single one is from our country. One of them is from Nepal, another from Africa. The rest are virtually all from Central America.'

'If that is so,' Abhijit asked, 'how do they survive here? I mean, does the soil here have . . .?'

'No. These plants have nothing to do with the soil.'

14

'No?'

'No. They do not derive sustenance from the soil. Just as human beings can survive anywhere in the world as long as they are fed properly, so can these plants. Adequate and appropriate food is all they need, no matter where they are kept.'

Kanti Babu stopped before a glass case. In it was an extraordinary plant. Its leaves were about two inches long, their edges were white and were serrated, as if they had teeth.

The front of the case had a kind of door, though it was big enough only for the mouth of the bottle to go through. It was bolted from outside. Kanti Babu unbolted it. Then he removed the stopper from the bottle and quickly slipped the bottle through the 'door'. A house-cricket leapt out into the case. Kanti Babu removed the bottle and replaced the stopper. Then he pushed the bolt back into place.

The house-cricket moved restlessly for a few seconds. Then it went and sat on a leaf. At once, the leaf folded itself and caught the insect. To my complete amazement, I saw that the two sets of teeth had closed in and clamped on each other so tightly that the poor house-cricket had no chance of escaping. I had no idea nature could set such a strange, horrific trap. Certainly, I had never seen anything like it before.

Abhijit was the first to speak. 'Is there any guarantee,' he asked hoarsely, 'that the insect would sit on a leaf?'

'Of course. You see, the plant exudes a smell that attracts insects. This plant is called the Venus fly trap. I brought it from Central America. If you go through books on botany, you may find pictures of this plant.'

I was still staring in speechless amazement at the house-cricket. At first, it was struggling to get out, but now it was just lying in its trap, quite lifeless. The pressure from the leaf's 'teeth' appeared to be getting stronger. This plant was every bit as violent as a gecko.

Abhijit laughed dryly. 'If I could keep such a plant in my house, I'd be safe from insects. At least, I wouldn't have to use DDT to kill cockroaches!'

'No, this particular plant couldn't eat—and digest—a cockroach. Its leaves are too small. There's a different plant to deal with cockroaches. Come this way,' invited Kanti Babu.

The next glass case had a plant whose long, large leaves looked like those of a lily. Each leaf had a strange object hanging from its tip. It looked like a pitcher-shaped bag, complete with a lid. I had already seen its picture. It was not difficult to recognize it.

'This,' Kanti Babu declared, 'is nepenthes, or a pitcher plant. It requires bigger creatures to survive. When I first found it, there were the crushed remains of a small bird in one of those pitchers.'

'Oh my God!' Abhijit exclaimed. The faint contempt his tone had held earlier was quickly disappearing. 'What does it eat now?'

'Cockroaches, caterpillars, even butterflies. Once I found a rat in my rat-trap. I fed it to that plant, it didn't seem to mind. But sometimes these plants eat more than they can digest, and then they die. They're a greedy lot. There are times when they just can't figure out how much strain their own digestive system can bear!'

We moved on to look at other plants, our astonishment mounting higher. There were butterwort, sundew, bladderwort, arozia—plants whose pictures I had seen. But the others were totally new, completely astounding, perfectly incredible. Kanti Babu had collected at least twenty different species of carnivorous plants, some of which, he said, were not included in any other collection in the world.

The prettiest amongst these was the sundew. It had fine strands of hair around its leaves. A droplet glistened on the tip of each hair. Kanti Babu tied a tiny piece of meat—no bigger than a peppercorn—to a thread and took it close to a leaf. We could see, even from a distance, all the hair rise at once, grasping at the piece of meat greedily. But Kanti Babu removed his hand before the meat could be taken.

'If it did get that piece of meat, it would have crushed it, just like the fly trap. Then it would have absorbed whatever nourishment it could get, and rejected the chewed pulp. Not really that different from the way you and I eat meat, is it?'

We left the shed and came out to the garden. The shirish tree was casting a long shadow. I looked at my watch. It was half past four.

'You will find mention of most of these plants in your books,' said Kanti Babu. 'But no one knows about the one I am now going to show you. It will never get written about, unless I write about it myself. In fact, I called you over here really to show you this plant. Come, Parimal. Come with me, Abhijit Babu.'

This time, Kanti Babu led the way to what looked like a factory behind the shirish tree. The door, made of tin, was locked. There was a window on either side. Kanti Babu pushed one of these open, peered in, then withdrew. 'Have a look!' he said.

Abhijit and I placed ourselves at the window. The room was only partially lit by the sunlight that came in through two skylights set high on the opposite wall.

The object the room contained hardly looked like a plant, or a tree. As a matter of fact, it was more like a weird animal— one with large, thick tentacles. A closer look, however, did reveal a trunk. It rose from the ground by several feet to end at what might be described as a head. About eighteen inches below this head, surrounding it, were tentacles. I counted them. There were seven.

The bark of the tree was pale, but it had round brown marks all over.

The tentacles were hanging limply, resting on the ground. The whole object appeared lifeless. Yet, I could feel my flesh creep.

I noticed something else, as my eyes got used to the dark. The floor around the plant was littered with the feathers of some bird.

Neither Abhijit nor I could speak. How long the silence continued, I cannot tell. It was Kanti Babu's voice that broke it. 'The plant is asleep at this moment. It's almost time for it to wake up.'

'Is it really a plant?' Abhijit asked incredulously.

'Well, it has grown out of the ground. What else would you call it? It doesn't, however, behave like a plant. No botanical reference book, or encyclopaedia, could give you a suitable name for it.'

'What do you call it?'

'Septopus. Because it has seven tentacles.'

We began walking back to the house.

'Where did you find it?' I asked.

'There is a dense forest near Lake Nicaragua in Central America. That's where I found it.'

'You must have had to search the area pretty thoroughly?'

'Yes, but I knew that the plant was available there. You haven't heard of Professor Dunston, have you? He was a botanist and an explorer. He died in Central America, looking for rare plants. But his death was quite mysterious. No one ever found his body, no one knows exactly how he died. This particular plant was mentioned in his diary, towards the very end.

'So I went to Nicaragua at the first opportunity. When I got to Guatemala, I heard people talking about this plant. They called it the Satan's Tree. Eventually, I saw a number of these plants. I saw them eat monkeys, armadillos, and other animals. Then, after many days of careful searching, I found a small sapling and brought it with me. You can see how big it has grown in two years.'

'What does it eat here?'

'Whatever I give it. Sometimes I catch rats in my trap to

feed it. Prayag has been told to get hold of dogs and cats that get run over. It has eaten those, too. Sometimes I give it the same things that you and I would eat—chicken or goat. Recently, its appetite seems to have grown quite a lot. I can't keep up with it. When it wakes up in the evening, it gets really restless. Yesterday, something happened . . . it was just terrible. Prayag had gone to feed it a chicken. It has to be fed in much the same way as an elephant. The head of this plant has a kind of lid. First of all, it opens its lid. Then it grabs the food with one of its tentacles, as an elephant picks up its food with its trunk, and places it into the opening in the head. After that, it remains quiet for a while. When it starts swinging its tentacles, that means it wants to eat some more.

'So far, a couple of chickens or a lamb was proving to be quite sufficient for a day's meal. Things have changed since yesterday. Prayag fed it the second chicken, shut the door and came away. When the plant gets restless, it strikes its tentacles against the floor, which creates a noise. Prayag heard this noise even after the second chicken had disappeared. So he went back to investigate.

'I was in my room at the time, making entries in my diary. A sudden scream made me come running here to see what was going on. What I saw was horrible. The plant had grabbed Prayag's right hand with a tentacle. Prayag was trying desperately to free his hand, but another tentacle was raised and making its way to him.

'I had to pick up my stick and strike at that tentacle with all my might, and then put both my arms round Prayag to pull him back. Yes, I rescued him all right, but what I saw the plant do next left me feeling positively alarmed. It had managed to tear off a piece of flesh from Prayag's hand. I saw it remove the lid on its head and put it in. I saw it with my own eyes!'

We had reached the front veranda once again. Kanti Babu sat down on a chair. Then he took out a handkerchief and wiped his forehead. 'I had no idea that the Septopus would wish to attack a human being. But now . . . since there has been such an indication . . . I don't have any option. I have got to kill it. I decided to do so immediately after I saw Prayag being attacked, and I put poison in its food. But that plant has such amazing intelligence, it picked the food up with a tentacle, but threw it away instantly. Now the only thing I can do is shoot it. Parimal, now do you understand why I called you here?'

I remained quiet for a few moments. Then I said, 'Do you know for sure that it will die if it's shot?'

'No, I cannot be sure. But I do believe that it has a brain. Besides, I have proof that it can think and judge. I have gone near it so many times, it has never attacked me. It seems to know me well, just as a dog knows its master. It dislikes Prayag because sometimes Prayag has, in the past, teased it and played tricks on it. He has tempted it with food, then refused to feed. I have seen Prayag take its food close to its tentacles, then withdraw it before the plant could grasp it. Yes, it most definitely has a brain, and that is where it should be, in its head. You must aim and fire at the spot from which those tentacles have grown.'

This time, Abhijit spoke. 'That's not a problem!' he said casually. 'It will only take a minute. Parimal, get your gun.'

Kanti Babu raised a hand to stop Abhijit. 'If the prey is asleep, is it right to kill it? What does your hunting code say, Parimal?'

'It is quite unethical to kill a sleeping animal. In this case, the prey is incapable of running away. There is no question of killing it until it wakes up.'

Kanti Babu rose and poured tea out of a flask. The Septopus woke within fifteen minutes of our finishing the tea.

Badshah, in the living room, had grown increasingly restive while we were talking. The sound of his keening and scratching noises made both Abhijit and me jump up and go inside. We found Badshah straining at his leash and trying to bite his collar. Abhijit began to calm him down, but at that moment, we heard a swishing noise coming from the factory. It was accompanied by a sharp, pungent smell. It is difficult to describe it. When I was a child, I had had my tonsils removed. Before the operation, I had smelt chloroform. It was somewhat similar.

Kanti Babu swept into the living room. 'Come on, it's time!' he said.

'What is that smell?' I asked.

'It's coming from the Septopus. That's the smell it spreads to attract ani . . .'

Kanti Babu could not finish. Badshah broke free with a mighty pull at the leash, knocked Abhijit out of the way, and leapt in the direction of the factory, to look for the source of the smell.

'Oh God, no!' cried Abhijit, picking himself up and running after his dog.

I picked up my loaded gun and followed him quickly. When I got there only a few seconds later, Badshah was springing up to the open window, ignoring Abhijit's futile attempts to stop him. Then he jumped into the room.

Kanti Babu ran to unlock the door. We heard the agonized screams of the Rampur hound even as Kanti Babu turned the key in the lock.

We tumbled into the room, to witness a horrible sight. One tentacle was not enough this time. The Septopus was wrapping a second, and then a third tentacle around Badshah, in a deadly embrace.

Kanti Babu shouted, 'Don't get any closer, either of you. Parimal, fire!'

I raised my gun, but another voice yelled: 'Stop!'

Now I realized how precious his dog was to Abhijit. He paid no attention to Kanti Babu's warning. I saw him run to the plant, and clutch with both hands one of the three tentacles that were wrapped around Badshah.

What followed froze my blood.

All three tentacles left Badshah immediately and attacked Abhijit. And the remaining four, perhaps aroused by the prospect of tasting human blood, rose from the ground, swaying greedily.

Kanti Babu spoke again. 'Come on, shoot. Look, there's the head!'

A lid from the top of the head was being slowly removed, revealing a dark cavern. The tentacles, lifting and carrying Abhijit with them, were moving towards that yawning gap.

Abhijit's face looked deathly pale, his eyes were bursting out of their sockets.

At any moment of crisis, I had noticed before, my nerves would become perfectly steady and calm, as if by magic.

I raised my gun, took aim and fired at the head of the Septopus, between two brown circular marks in the centre. My hands did not tremble, and my bullet found its mark.

In the next instant, I remember, thick red blood began spurting out of the wounded plant, gushing forth like a fountain. And the tentacles released Abhijit, hanging low, dropping down to the ground, still and lifeless. The last thing I remember is the smell, which suddenly grew ten times stronger, overwhelming my senses, blocking out consciousness, numbing my thoughts . . .

*

Four months had passed since that day. I had only recently resumed writing. My novel was still incomplete.

It had proved impossible to save Badshah. But Abhijit had already found a mastiff and a Tibetan pup. He was looking for another Rampur hound, I had learnt. Two of his ribs were fractured as a result of his encounter with the Septopus. It took him two months to recover.

Kanti Babu visited me yesterday. He was thinking of getting rid of all his plants that ate insects, he said.

'It might be a good idea to experiment with vegetables, don't you think? I mean, I could grow courgettes, gourds, marrows, things like that. If you like, I can give you some of my old plants. You did so much for me, I am very grateful to you. Say I give you a nepenthes? It can at least take care of the insects in your house . . .?'

'No, no!' I interrupted him. 'If you wish to get rid of those plants, do. Just throw them out. I don't need a plant to catch my insects.'

This last remark received wholehearted support from the gecko sprawled over the calendar.

'Tik, tik, tik!' it said.

Translated by Gopa Majumdar

Bonku Babu's Friend

No one had ever seen Bonku Babu get cross. To tell the truth, it was difficult to imagine what he might say or do, if one day he did get angry.

It was not as if there was never any reason for him to lose his temper. For the last twenty-two years, Bonku Babu had taught geography and Bengali at the Kankurgachhi Primary School. Every year, a new batch of students replaced the old one, but old or new, the tradition of teasing poor Bonku Babu continued among all the students. Some drew his picture on the blackboard; others put glue on his chair; or, on the night of Kali Puja, they lit a 'chasing-rocket' and set it off to chase him.

Bonku Babu did not get upset by any of this. Only

sometimes, he cleared his throat and said, 'Shame on you, boys!'

One of the reasons for maintaining his calm was simply that he could not afford to do otherwise. If he did lose his temper and left his job in a fit of pique, he knew how difficult it would then be to find another, at his age. Another reason was that in every class, there were always a few good students, even if the rest of the class was full of pranksters. Teaching this handful of good boys was so rewarding that, to Bonku Babu, that alone made life as a teacher worth living. At times, he invited those boys to his house, offered them snacks and told them tales of foreign lands and exciting adventures. He told them about life in Africa, the discovery of the North Pole, the fish in Brazil that ate human flesh, and about Atlantis, the continent submerged under the sea. He was a good storyteller, he had his audience enthralled.

During the weekend, Bonku Babu went to the lawyer, Sripati Majumdar's house, to spend the evenings with other regulars. On a number of occasions, he had come back thinking, 'Enough, never again!' The reason was simply that he could put up with the pranks played by the boys in his school, but when grown, even middle aged men started making fun of him, it became too much to bear. At these meetings that Sripati Babu hosted in the evenings, nearly everyone poked fun at Bonku Babu, sometimes bringing his endurance to breaking point.

Only the other day—less than two months ago—they were talking about ghosts. Usually, Bonku Babu kept his mouth shut. That day, for some unknown reason, he opened it and declared that he was not afraid of ghosts. That was all. But it was enough to offer a golden opportunity to the others. On his way back later that night, Bonku Babu was attacked by a 'spook'. As he was passing a tamarind tree, a tall, thin figure leapt down and landed on his back. As it happened, this apparition had smeared black ink all over itself, possibly at the suggestion of someone at the meeting.

Bonku Babu did not feel frightened. But he was injured. For three days, his neck ached. Worst of all—his new kurta was torn and it had black stains all over. What kind of a joke was this?

Other 'jokes', less serious in nature, were often played on him. His umbrella or his shoes were hidden sometimes; at others, a paan would be filled with dust instead of masala, and handed to him; or he would be forced to sing.

Even so, Bonku Babu had to come to these meetings. If he didn't, what would Sripati Babu think? Not only was he a very important man in the village, but he couldn't do without Bonku Babu. According to Sripati Majumdar, it was essential to have a butt of ridicule, who could provide amusement to all. Or what was the point in having a meeting? So Bonku Babu was fetched, even if he tried to keep away.

*

On one particular day, the topic of conversation was high-flying—in other words, they were talking of satellites. Soon after sunset, a moving point of light had been seen in the northern sky. A similar light was seen three months ago, which had led to much speculation. In the end, it turned out to be a Russian satellite, called Khotka—or was it Phoshka? Anyway, this satellite was supposed to be going round the earth at a height of 400 miles, and providing a lot of valuable information to scientists.

That evening, Bonku Babu was the first to spot that strange light. Then he called Nidhu Babu and showed it to him. However, he arrived at the meeting to find that Nidhu Babu had coolly claimed full credit for being the first to see it, and was boasting a great deal. Bonku Babu said nothing.

No one knew much about satellites, but there was nothing to stop them from offering their views. Said Chandi Babu, 'You can say what you like, but I don't think we should waste our time worrying about satellites. Somebody sees a point of light in some obscure corner of the sky, and the press gets all excited about it. Then we read a report, say how clever it all is, have a chat about it in our living rooms, perhaps while we casually chew a paan, and behave as if we have achieved something. Humbug!'

Ramkanai countered this remark. He was still young. 'No, it may not be any of us here, but it is human achievement, surely? And a great achievement, at that.'

'Oh, come off it! Of course it's a human achievement . . . who'd build a satellite except men? You wouldn't expect a bunch of monkeys to do that, would you?'

'All right,' said Nidhu Babu, 'let's not talk of satellites.

After all, it's just a machine, going round the earth, they say. No different from a spinning top. A top would start spinning if you got it going; or a fan would start to rotate if you pressed a switch. A satellite's the same. But think of a rocket. That can't be dismissed so easily, can it?'

Chandi Babu wrinkled his nose. 'A rocket? Why, what good is a rocket? All right, if one was made here in our country, took off from the maidan in Calcutta, and we could all go and buy tickets to watch the show . . . well then, that would be nice. But . . .'

'You're right,' Ramkanai agreed. 'A rocket has no meaning for us here.'

Bhairav Chakravarty spoke next. 'Suppose some creature from a different planet arrived on earth . . . ?'

'So what? Even if it did, you and I would never be able to see it.'

'Yes, that's true enough.'

Everyone turned their attention to their cups of tea. There did not seem to be anything left to be said. After a few moments of silence, Bonku Babu cleared his throat and said gently, 'Suppose . . . suppose they came here?'

Nidhu Babu feigned total amazement. 'Hey, Bunkum wants to say something! What did you say, Bunkum? Who's going to come here? Where from?'

Bonku Babu repeated his words, his tone still gentle: 'Suppose someone from a different planet came here?'

As was his wont, Bhairav Chakravarty slapped Bonku Babu's back loudly and rudely, grinned and said, 'Bravo!

What a thing to say! Where is a creature from another planet going to land? Not Moscow, not London, not New York, not even Calcutta, but here? In Kankurgachhi? You do think big, don't you?'

Bonku Babu fell silent. But several questions rose in his mind. Was it really impossible? If an alien had to visit the earth, would it really matter where it arrived first? It might not aim to go straight to any other part of the world. All right, it was highly unlikely that such a thing would happen in Kankurgachhi, but who was to say for sure that it could not happen at all?

Sripati Babu was silent so far. Now, as he shifted in his seat, everyone looked at him. He put his cup down and spoke knowledgeably: 'Look, if someone from a different planet does come to earth, I can assure you that he will not come to this godforsaken place. Those people are no fools. It is my belief that they are sahibs, and they will land in some Western country, where all the sahibs live. Understand?'

Everyone agreed, with the sole exception of Bonku Babu.

Chandi Babu decided to take things a bit further. He nudged Nidhu Babu silently, pointed at Bonku Babu and spoke innocently, 'Why, I think Bonku is quite right. Isn't it natural that aliens should want to come to a place where there's a man like our Bonkubihari? If they wanted to take away a specimen, could they find anything better?'

'No, I don't think so!' Nidhu Babu joined in. 'Consider his looks, not to mention his brains . . . yes, Bunkum is the ideal specimen!'

'Right. Suitable for keeping in a museum. Or a zoo,' Ramkanai chipped in.

Bonku Babu did not reply, but wondered silently: if anyone were to look for a specimen, weren't the others just as suitable? Look at Sripati Babu. His chin was so much like a camel's. And that Bhairav Chakravarty, his eyes were like the eyes of a tortoise. Nidhu Babu looked like a mole, Ramkanai like a goat, and Chandi Babu like a flittermouse. If a zoo really had to be filled up . . .

Tears sprang to his eyes. Bonku Babu had come to the meeting hoping, for once, to enjoy himself. That was clearly not to be. He could not stay here any longer. He rose to his feet.

'Why, what's the matter? Are you leaving already?' Sripati Babu asked, sounding concerned.

'Yes, it's getting late.'

'Late? Pooh, it's not late at all. Anyway, tomorrow is a holiday. Sit down, have some more tea.'

'No, thank you. I must go. I have some papers to mark. Namaskar.'

'Take care, Bonkuda,' warned Ramkanai, 'it's a moonless night, remember. And it's a Saturday. Very auspicious for ghosts and spooks!'

*

Bonku Babu saw the light when he was about halfway through the bamboo grove. Poncha Ghosh owned that entire area. Bonku Babu was not carrying a torch or a lantern. There was no need for it. It was too cold for snakes to be out and about, and he knew his way very well. Normally, not many people took this route, but it meant a short cut for him.

In the last few minutes he had become aware of something unusual. At first, he could not put his finger on it. Somehow, things were different tonight. What was wrong? What was missing? Suddenly, he realized that the crickets were silent. Not one was chirping. Usually, the crickets sounded louder as he delved deeper into the bamboo grove. Today, there was only an eerie silence. What had happened to the crickets? Were they all asleep?

Puzzled, Bonku Babu walked another twenty yards, and then saw the light. At first, he thought a fire had broken out. Bang in the middle of the bamboo grove, in the clearing near a small pond, quite a large area was glowing pink. A dull light shone on every branch and every leaf. Down below, the ground behind the pond was lit by a much stronger pink light. But it was not a fire, for it was still.

Bonku Babu kept moving.

Soon, his ears began ringing. He felt as if someone was humming loudly—a long, steady noise—there was no way he could stop it. Bonku Babu broke into goosepimples, but an irrepressible curiosity drove him further forward.

As he went past a cluster of bamboo stems, an object came into view. It looked like a giant glass bowl, turned upside-down, covering the pond completely. It was through its translucent shade that a strong, yet gentle pink light was shining out, to turn the whole area radiant.

Not even in a dream had Bonku Babu witnessed such a strange scene.

After staring at it for a few stunned minutes, he noticed that although the object was still, it did not appear to be lifeless. There was the odd flicker; and the glass mound was rising and falling, exactly as one's chest heaves while breathing.

He took a few steps to get a better look, but felt suddenly as if an electric current had passed through his body. In the next instant, he was rendered completely immobile. His hands and feet were tied with an invisible rope. There was no strength left in his body. He could move neither forward, nor backward.

A few moments later, Bonku Babu—still standing stiffly on the same spot—saw that the object gradually stopped 'breathing'. At once, his ears ceased ringing and the humming stopped. A second later, a voice spoke, shattering the silence of the night. It sounded human, but was extraordinarily thin.

'Milipi-ping kruk! Milipi-ping kruk!' it said loudly.

Bonku Babu gave a start. What did it mean? What language was this? And where was the speaker?

The next words the voice spoke made his heart jump again.

'Who are you? Who are you?'

Why, these were English words! Was the question addressed to him? Bonku Babu swallowed. 'I am Bonkubihari Datta, sir. Bonkubihari Datta,' he replied.

'Are you English? Are you English?' the voice went on.

'No, sir!' Bonku Babu shouted back. 'Bengali, sir. A Bengali kayastha.'

This was followed by a short pause. Then the voice came back, speaking clearly: 'Namaskar!'

Bonku Babu heaved a sigh of relief and returned the greeting. 'Namaskar!' he said, suddenly realizing that the invisible bonds that were holding him tightly had disappeared. He was free to run away, but he did not. Now his astounded eyes could see that a portion of the glass mound was sliding to one side, opening out like a door.

Through that door emerged a head—like a plain, smooth ball—and then the body of a weird creature.

Its arms and legs were amazingly thin. With the exception of its head, its whole body was covered by a shiny, pink outfit. Instead of ears, it had a tiny hole on each side of its head. On its face were two holes where it should have had a nose, and another gaping hole instead of a mouth. There was no sign of hair anywhere. Its eyes were round and bright yellow. They appeared to be glowing in the dark.

The creature walked slowly towards Bonku Babu, and stopped only a few feet away. Then it gave him a steady, unblinking stare. Automatically, Bonku Babu found himself folding his hands. Having stared at him for nearly a minute, it spoke in the same voice that sounded more like a flute than anything else: 'Are you human?'

'Yes.'

'Is this Earth?'

'Yes.'

'Ah, I thought as much. My instruments are not working properly. I was supposed to go to Pluto. I wasn't sure where I had landed, so I spoke to you first in the language they use on Pluto. When you didn't reply, I could tell I had landed on Earth. A complete waste of time and effort. It happened once before. Instead of going to Mars, I veered off and went to Jupiter. Delayed me by a whole day, it did. Heh heh heh!'

Bonku Babu did not know what to say. He was feeling quite uncomfortable, for the creature had started to press his arms and legs with its long, slim fingers. When it finished, it introduced itself. 'I am Ang, from the planet Craneus. A far superior being than man.'

What! This creature, barely four feet tall, with such thin limbs and weird face, was superior to man? Bonku Babu nearly burst out laughing. Ang read his mind immediately. 'There's no need to be so sceptical. I can prove it. How many languages do you know?'

Bonku Babu scratched his head. 'Bengali, English and . . . er . . . Hindi . . . a little Hindi . . . I mean . . .'

'You mean two and a half?'

'Yes.'

'I know 14,000. There isn't a single language in your solar system that I do not know. I also know thirty-one languages spoken on planets outside your system. I have been to twenty-five of them. How old are you?'

'I am fifty.'

'I am 833. Do you eat animals?'

Bonku Babu had had meat curry only recently, on the day of Kali Puja. How could he deny it?

'We stopped eating meat several centuries ago,' Ang informed him. 'Before that, we used to eat the flesh of most creatures. I might have eaten you.'

Bonku Babu swallowed hard.

'Take a look at this!' Ang offered him a small object. It looked like a pebble. Bonku Babu touched it for an instant, and felt the same electric current pass through his body. He withdrew his hand at once.

Ang smiled. 'A little while ago, you could not move an inch. Do you know why? It was only because I had this little thing in my hand. It would stop anyone from getting closer. Nothing can be more effective than this in making an enemy perfectly powerless, without actually hurting him physically.'

Now Bonku Babu felt genuinely taken aback.

Ang said, 'Is there any place that you have wished to visit, or a scene that you have longed to see, but never could?'

Bonku Babu thought: why, the whole world remained to be seen! He taught geography, but what had he seen except a few villages and towns in Bengal? There was so much in Bengal itself that he had never had the chance to see. The snow-capped Himalayas, the sea in Digha, the forests in the Sunderbans, or even that famous banyan tree in Shibpur.

However, he mentioned none of these thoughts to Ang. 'There is so much I would like to see,' he finally admitted, 'but most of all . . . I think I would like to visit the North Pole. I come from a warm country, you see, so . . .'

Ang took out a small tube, one end of which was covered by a piece of glass. 'Take a look through this!' Ang invited. Bonku Babu peered through the glass, and felt all his hair rise. Could this be true? Could he really believe his eyes? Before him stretched an endless expanse of snow, dotted with large mounds, also covered with ice and snow. Above him, against a deep blue sky, all the colours of a rainbow were forming different patterns, changing every second. The Aurora Borealis! What was that? An igloo. There was a group of polar bears. Wait, there was another animal. A strange, peculiar creature . . . Yes! It was a walrus. There were two of them, in fact. And they were fighting. Their tusks were bared—large as radishes—and they were attacking each other. Streams of bright red blood were running on the soft white snow . . .

It was December, and Bonku Babu was looking at an area hidden under layers of snow. Still, he broke into a sweat.

'What about Brazil? Don't you wish to go there?' asked Ang.

Bonku Babu remembered instantly—piranhas, those deadly carnivorous fish! Amazing. How did this Ang know what he would like to see?

Bonku Babu peered through the tube again. He could see a dense forest. Only a little scattered sunlight had crept in through the almost impenetrable foliage. There was a huge tree, and hanging from a branch . . . what was that? Oh God, he could never even have imagined the size of that snake. Anaconda! The name flashed through his mind. Yes, he had read somewhere about it. It was said to be much, much larger than a python.

But where was the fish? Oh, here was a canal. Crocodiles lined its banks, sleeping in the sun. One of them moved. It was going to go into the water. Splash! Bonku Babu could almost hear the noise. But . . . what was that? The crocodile had jumped out of the water very quickly. Was . . . could it be the same one that went in only a few seconds ago? With his eyes nearly popping out, Bonku Babu noted that there was virtually no flesh left on the belly of the crocodile, bones were showing through clearly. Attached to the remaining flesh were five fish with amazingly sharp teeth and a monstrous appetite. Pirahnas!

Bonku Babu could not bear to watch any more. His limbs were trembling, his head reeled painfully.

'Now do you believe that we are superior?' Ang wanted to know.

Bonku Babu ran his tongue over his parched lips. 'Yes. Oh yes. Certainly. Of course!' he croaked.

'Very well. Look, I have been watching you. And I have examined your arms and legs. You belong to a much inferior species. There is no doubt about that. However, as human beings go, you are not too bad. I mean, you are a good man. But you have a major fault. You are much too meek and mild. That is why you have made so little progress in life. You must always speak up against injustice, and protest if anyone hurts or insults you without any provocation. To take it quietly is wrong, not just for man, but for any creature anywhere. Anyway, it was nice to have met you, although I wasn't really supposed to be here at this time. There's no point in wasting more time on your Earth. I had better go.'

'Goodbye, Mr Ang. I am very glad to have made your . . .'

Bonku Babu could not complete his sentence. In less than a second, almost before he could grasp what was happening, Ang had leapt into his spaceship and risen over Poncha Ghosh's bamboo grove. Then he vanished completely. Bonku Babu realized that the crickets had started chirping again. It was really quite late.

Bonku Babu resumed walking towards his house, his mind still in a wondrous haze. Slowly, the full implications of the recent events began to sink in. A man—no, it was not a man, it was Ang—came here from some unknown planet, who knew if anyone had ever heard its name, and spoken to him. How extraordinary! How completely incredible! There were billions and billions of people in the world. But who got the chance to have this wonderful experience? Bonkubihari Datta, teacher of geography and Bengali in the Kankurgachhi Primary School. No one else. From today, at least in this particular matter, he was unique, in the whole wide world.

Bonku Babu realized that he was no longer walking. With a spring in every step, he was actually dancing.

The next day was a Sunday. Everyone had turned up for their usual meeting at Sripati Babu's house. There was a report in the local paper about a strange light, but it was only a small report. This light had been seen by a handful of people in only two places in Bengal. It was therefore being put in the same category as sightings of flying saucers.

Tonight, Poncha Ghosh was also present at the meeting. He was talking about his bamboo grove. All the bamboo around the pond in the middle of the wood had shed all their leaves. It was not unusual for leaves to drop in winter, but for so many plants to become totally bare overnight was certainly a remarkable occurrence. Everyone was talking about it, when suddenly Bhairav Chakravarty said, 'Why is Bonku so late today?'

Everyone stopped talking. So far, no one had noticed Bonku Babu's absence.

'I don't think Bunkum will show his face here today. Didn't he get an earful yesterday when he tried to open his mouth?' said Nidhu Babu.

'No, no,' Sripati Babu sounded concerned, 'we must have Bonku. Ramkanai, go and see if you can get hold of him.'

'Okay, I'll go as soon as I've had my tea,' replied Ramkanai and was about to take a sip, when Bonku Babu entered the room. No, to say 'entered' would be wrong. It was as if a small hurricane swept in, in the guise of a short, dark man, throwing everyone into stunned silence.

Then it swung into action. Bonku Babu burst into a guffaw, and laughed uproariously for a whole minute, the like of which no one had heard before, not even Bonku Babu himself.

When he could finally stop, he cleared his throat and began speaking:

'Friends! I have great pleasure in telling you that this is the last time you will see me at your meeting. The only reason I am here today is simply that I would like to tell you a few things before I go. Number one—this is for all of you—you speak a great deal of rubbish. Only fools talk of things they don't know anything about. Number two—this is for Chandi Babu—at your age, hiding other people's shoes and umbrellas is not just childish, but totally wrong. Kindly bring my umbrella and brown canvas shoes to my house tomorrow. Nidhu Babu, if you call me Bunkum, I will call you Nitwit, and you must learn to live with that. And Sripati Babu, you are an important man, of course you must have hangers-on. But let me tell you, from today you can count me out. If you like, I can send my cat, it's quite good at licking feet. And . . . oh, you are here as well, Poncha Babu! Let me inform you and everyone else, that last night, an Ang arrived from the planet Craneus and landed on the pond in your bamboo grove. We had a long chat. The man . . . sorry, the Ang . . . was most amiable.'

Bonku Babu finished his speech and slapped Bhairav Chakravarty's back so hard that he choked. Then he made his exit, walking swiftly, his head held high.

In the same instant, the cup fell from Ramkanai's hand, shattering to pieces, splattering hot tea on most of the others.

Translated by Gopa Majumdar

Bipin Chowdhury's Lapse of Memory

Every Monday, on his way back from work, Bipin Chowdhury would drop in at Kalicharan's in New Market to buy books. Crime stories, ghost stories and thrillers. He had to buy at least five at a time to last him through the week. He lived alone, was not a good mixer, had few friends, and didn't like spending time in idle chat. Those who called in the evening got through their business quickly and left. Those who didn't show signs of leaving would be told around eight o'clock by Bipin Babu that he was under doctor's orders to have dinner at eight-thirty. After dinner he would rest for half an hour and then turn in with a book. This was a routine which had persisted unbroken for years.

Today, at Kalicharan's, Bipin Babu had the feeling that

someone was observing him from close quarters. He turned round and found himself looking at a round-faced meek-looking man who now broke into a smile.

'I don't suppose you recognize me.'

Bipin Babu felt ill at ease. It didn't seem that he had ever encountered this man before. The face seemed quite unfamiliar.

'But you're a busy man. You must meet all kinds of people all the time.'

'Have we met before?' asked Bipin Babu.

The man looked greatly surprised. 'We met every day for a whole week. I arranged for a car to take you to the Hudroo falls in 1958 in Ranchi. My name is Parimal Ghose.'

'Ranchi?'

Now Bipin Babu realized that it was not he but this man who was making a mistake. Bipin Babu had never been to Ranchi. He had been at the point of going several times, but had never made it. He smiled and said, 'Do you know who I am?'

The man raised his eyebrows, bit his tongue and said, 'Do I know you? Who doesn't know Bipin Chowdhury?'

Bipin Babu now turned towards the bookshelves and said, 'Still you're making a mistake. One often does. I've never been to Ranchi.'

The man now laughed aloud.

'What are you saying, Mr Chowdhury? You had a fall in Hudroo and cut your right knee. I brought you iodine. I had fixed up a car for you to go to Netarhat the next day, but you couldn't because of the pain in the knee. Can't you recall anything? Someone else you know was also in Ranchi at that time. Mr Dinesh Mukerjee. You stayed in a bungalow. You said you didn't like hotel food and would prefer to have your meals cooked by a bawarchi. Mr Mukerjee stayed with his sister. You had a big argument about the moon landing, remember? I'll tell you more: you always carried a bag with your books in it on your sightseeing trips. Am I right or not?'

Bipin Babu spoke quietly, his eyes still on the books.

'Which month in fifty-eight are you talking about?'

The man said, 'Just before the pujas. October.'

'No, sir,' said Bipin Babu. 'I spent puja in fifty-eight with a friend in Kanpur. You're making a mistake. Good day.'

But the man didn't go, nor did he stop talking.

'Very strange. One evening I had tea with you on the veranda of your bungalow. You spoke about your family. You said you had no children, and that you had lost your wife ten years ago. Your only brother had died insane, which is why you didn't want to visit the mental hospital in Ranchi . . .'

When Bipin Babu had paid for the books and was leaving the shop, the man was still looking at him in utter disbelief.

Bipin Babu's car was safely parked in Bertram Street by the Lighthouse cinema. He told the driver as he got into the car, 'Just drive by the Ganga, will you, Sitaram.' Driving up the Strand Road, Bipin Babu regretted having paid so much attention to the intruder. He had never been to Ranchi—no question about it. It was inconceivable that he should forget such an incident which took place only six or seven years ago. He had an excellent memory. Unless—Bipin Babu's head reeled.

Unless he was losing his mind.

But how could that be? He was working daily in his office. It was a big firm, and he had a responsible job. He wasn't aware of anything ever going seriously wrong. Only today he had spoken for half an hour at an important meeting. And yet . . .

And yet that man knew a great deal about him. How? He even seemed to know some intimate details. The bag of books, his wife's death, brother's insanity . . . The only mistake was about his having gone to Ranchi. Not a mistake; a deliberate lie. In fifty-eight, during the pujas, he was in Kanpur at his friend Haridas Bagchi's place. All Bipin Babu had to do was write to—no, there was no way of writing to Haridas. Bipin Babu suddenly remembered that Haridas had not left his address.

But where was the need for proof? If it so happened that the police were trying to pin a crime on him which had taken place in Ranchi in fifty-eight, he might have needed to prove he hadn't been there. He himself was fully aware that he hadn't been to Ranchi—and that was that.

The river breeze was bracing, and yet a slight discomfort lingered in Bipin Babu's mind.

Around Hastings, Bipin Babu had the sudden notion of rolling up his trousers and taking a look at his right knee.

There was the mark of an old inch-long cut. It was impossible to tell when the injury had occurred. Had he never had a fall as a boy and cut his knee? He tried to recall such an incident, but couldn't.

Then Bipin Babu suddenly thought of Dinesh Mukerjee. The man had said that Dinesh was in Ranchi at the same time. The best thing surely would be to ask him. He lived quite near—in Beninandan Street. What about going right now? But then, if he had really never been to Ranchi, what would Dinesh think if Bipin Babu asked for a confirmation? He would probably conclude Bipin Babu was going nuts. No—it would be ridiculous to ask him. And he knew how ruthless Dinesh's sarcasm could be.

Sipping a cold drink in his air-conditioned living room, Bipin Babu felt at ease again. Such a nuisance the man was! He probably had nothing else to do, so he went about getting into other people's hair.

After dinner, snuggling in bed with one of the new thrillers, Bipin Babu forgot all about the man in New Market.

Next day, in the office, Bipin Babu noticed that with every passing hour, the previous day's encounter was occupying his mind more and more. That look of round-eyed surprise on that round face, the disbelieving snigger . . . If the man knew so much about the details of Bipin Babu's life, how could he be so wrong about the Ranchi trip?

Just before lunch—at five minutes to one—Bipin Babu couldn't check himself any more. He opened the phone book. He had to ring up Dinesh Mukerjee. It was better to settle the question over the phone; at least the embarrassment on his face wouldn't show.

Two-three-five-six-one-six.

Bipin Babu dialled the number.

'Hello.'

'Is that Dinesh? This is Bipin here.'

'Well, well—what's the news?'

'I just wanted to find out if you recalled an incident which took place in fifty-eight.'

'Fifty-eight? What incident?'

'Were you in Calcutta right through that year? That's the first thing I've got to know.'

'Wait just a minute . . . fifty-eight . . . just let me check in my diary.'

For a minute there was silence. Bipin Babu could feel that his heartbeat had gone up. He was sweating a little.

'Hello.'

'Yes.'

'I've got it. I had been out twice.'

'Where?'

'Once in February—nearby—to Krishnanagar to a nephew's wedding. And then . . . but you'd know about this one. The trip to Ranchi. You were there too. That's all. But what's all this sleuthing about?'

'No, I just wanted to—anyway, thanks.'

Bipin Babu slammed the receiver down and gripped his head with his hands. He felt his head swimming. A chill seemed to spread over his body. There were sandwiches in his tiffin box, but he didn't feel like eating them. He had lost his appetite. Completely.

After lunchtime, Bipin Babu realized that he couldn't possibly carry on sitting at his desk and working. This was the first time something like this had happened in his twenty-five years with the firm. He had a reputation for being a tireless, conscientious worker. The men who worked under him all held him in awe. In the worst moments of crisis, even when faced with the most acute problems, Bipin Babu had always kept his cool and weathered the storm. But today his head was in a whirl.

Back home at two-thirty, Bipin Babu shut himself up in his bedroom, lay down in bed and tried to gather his wits together. He knew that it was possible to lose one's memory through an injury to the head, but he didn't know of a single instance of someone remembering everything except one particular incident—and a fairly recent and significant one at that. He had always wanted to go to Ranchi; to have gone there, done things, and not to remember was something utterly impossible.

At seven, Bipin Babu's servant came and announced that Seth Girdhariprasad had come. A rich businessman—and a VIP—this Girdhariprasad. And he had come by appointment. But Bipin Babu was feeling so low that he had to tell his servant that it was not possible for him to leave his bed. To hell with VIPs.

At seven-thirty, the servant came again. Bipin Babu had just dozed off and was in the middle of an unpleasant dream when the servant's knock woke him up. Who was it this time? 'Chuni Babu, sir. Says it's very urgent.'

Bipin Babu knew what the urgency was. Chunilal was a childhood friend of his. He had fallen on bad times recently, and had been pestering Bipin Babu for a job. Bipin Babu had kept fobbing him off, but Chuni kept coming back. What a persistent bore.

Bipin Babu sent word that not only was it not possible for him to see Chuni now, but not in several weeks as well.

But as soon as the servant stepped out of the room, it struck Bipin Babu that Chuni might remember something about the fifty-eight trip. There was no harm in asking him.

He sped downstairs. Chuni had got up to leave. Seeing Bipin Babu, he turned around with a flicker of hope in his eyes.

Bipin Babu didn't beat about the bush.

'Listen, Chuni—I want to ask you something. You have a good memory, and you've been seeing me off and on for a long time. Just throw your mind back and tell me—did I go to Ranchi in fifty-eight?'

Chuni said, 'Fifty-eight? It must have been fifty-eight. Or was it 1959?'

'You're sure that I did go to Ranchi?'

Chuni's look of amazement was not unmixed with worry.

'D'you mean you have doubts about having gone at all?'

'Did I go? Do you remember clearly?'

Chuni was standing up; he now sat down on the sofa, fixed Bipin Babu with a long, hard stare and said, 'Bipin, have you taken to drugs or something? As far as I know, you had a clean record where such things were concerned. I know that old friendships don't mean much to you, but at least you had a good memory. You can't really mean that you've forgotten about the Ranchi trip?'

Bipin Babu had to turn away from Chuni's incredulous stare.

'D'you remember what my last job was?' asked Chunilal.

'Of course. You worked in a travel agency.'

'You remember that and you don't remember that it was I who fixed up your booking for Ranchi? I went to the station to see you off; one of the fans in your compartment was not working—I got an electrician to fix it. Have you forgotten everything? Whatever is the matter with you? You don't look too well, you know.'

Bipin Babu sighed and shook his head.

'I've been working too hard,' he said at last. 'That must be the reason. Must see about consulting a specialist.'

Doubtless it was Bipin Babu's condition which made Chunilal leave without mentioning anything about a job.

✦

Paresh Chanda was a young physician with a pair of bright eyes and a sharp nose. He became thoughtful when he heard about Bipin Babu's symptoms. 'Look, Dr Chanda,' said Bipin Babu desperately, 'you must cure me of this horrible illness. I can't tell you how it's affecting my work. There are so many kinds of drugs these days; isn't there something specific for such a complaint? I can have it sent from abroad if it's not to be had here. But I must be rid of these symptoms.'

Dr Chanda shook his head.

'You know what, Mr Chowdhury,' he said, 'I've never had to deal with a case such as yours. Frankly, this is quite outside my field of experience. But I have one suggestion. I don't know if it'll work, but it's worth a try. It can do no harm.'

Bipin Babu leaned forward anxiously.

'As far as I can make out,' said Dr Chanda, 'and I think you're of the same opinion—you have been to Ranchi, but due to some unknown reason, the entire episode has slipped out of your mind. What I suggest is that you go to Ranchi once again. The sight of the place may remind you of your trip. This is not impossible. More than that I cannot do at the moment. I'm prescribing a nerve tonic and a tranquillizer. Sleep is essential, or the symptoms will get more pronounced.'

It may have been the sleeping pill, and the advice the doctor gave, which made Bipin Babu feel somewhat better the next morning.

After breakfast, he rang up his office, gave some instructions, and then procured a first-class ticket to Ranchi for the same evening.

Getting off the train at Ranchi next morning, he realized at once that he had never been there before.

He came out of the station, hired a taxi and drove around the town for a while. It was clear that the streets, the buildings, the hotels, the bazaars, the Morabadi Hill were all unfamiliar—with none of these had he the slightest acquaintance. Would a trip to the Hudroo Falls help? He didn't believe so, but, at the same time, he didn't wish to leave with the feeling that he hadn't tried hard enough. So he arranged for a car and left for Hudroo in the afternoon.

At five o'clock the same afternoon in Hudroo, two Gujarati gentlemen from a group of picnickers discovered Bipin Babu lying unconscious beside a boulder. When the ministrations of the two gentlemen brought him around, the first thing Bipin Babu said was, 'I'm finished. There's no hope left.'

Next morning, Bipin Babu was back in Calcutta. He realized that there was truly no hope for him. Soon he would lose everything: his will to work, his confidence, his ability, his balance of mind. Was he going to end up in the asylum at Ranchi . . . ? Bipin Babu couldn't think any more.

Back home, he rang up Dr Chanda and asked him to come over. Then, after a shower, he got into bed with an icebag clamped to his head. Just then the servant brought him a letter which someone had left in the letter box. A greenish envelope with his name in red ink on it. Above the name it said 'Urgent and Confidential'. In spite of his condition, Bipin Babu had a feeling that he ought to go through the letter. He tore open the envelope and took out the letter. This is what he read—

Dear Bipin,
I had no idea that affluence would bring about the

kind of change in you that it has done. Was it so difficult for you to help out an old friend down on his luck? I have no money, so my resources are limited. What I have is imagination, a part of which I used in retribution of your unfeeling behaviour.

The man in New Market is a neighbour and acquaintance of mine and a capable actor who played the part I wrote for him. Dinesh Mukerjee has never been particularly well-disposed towards you: so he was quite willing to help. As for the mark on your knee, you will surely recall that you tripped on a rope in Chandpal Ghat back in 1939.

Well, you'll be all right again now. A novel I've written is being considered by a publisher. If he likes it enough, it'll see me through the next few months.
Yours,
Chunilal

When Dr Chanda came, Bipin Babu said, 'I'm fine. It all came back as soon as I got off the train at Ranchi.'

'A unique case,' said Dr Chanda. 'I shall certainly write about it in a medical journal.'

'The reason why I sent for you,' said Bipin Babu, 'is that I have a pain in the hip from a fall I had in Ranchi. If you could prescribe a painkiller . . . '

Translated by Satyajit Ray

The Two Magicians

'Five, six, seven, eight, nine, ten, eleven,' Surapati finished counting the trunks and turned towards his assistant, Anil. 'All right,' he said, 'have these loaded into the brake van. Just twenty-five minutes left.'

'I have checked your reservation, sir,' said Anil. 'It's a coupé. Both berths are reserved in your name. It'll be all right.' Then he smiled a little and added, 'The guard is a fan of yours. He's seen your show at the New Empire. Here, sir, come this way!'

The guard, Biren Bakshi, came forward with an outstretched hand and a broad smile. 'Do allow me,' he said, 'to shake the famous hand that has performed all those tricks that gave me so much joy. It is an honour indeed!'

One only had to look at any of Surapati Mondol's eleven trunks to realize who he was. Each bore the legend 'Mondol's Miracles' in large letters both on its sides and its lid. He needed no further introduction. It was barely two months since his last show at the New Empire Theatre in Calcutta, where a large audience, enchanted by his magic show, had expressed genuine appreciation through thunderous applause again and again. The newspapers, too, had carried rave reviews. The week-long show had to be extended to four, on popular demand. Eventually, Surapati had to promise the authorities another show over the Christmas break.

'If you need any help, do let me know,' said the guard as he ushered Surapati into his coupé. Surapati looked around and heaved a sigh of relief. He liked the little compartment.

'All right then, sir. May I take your leave?'

'Many thanks.'

The guard left. Surapati settled down by the window and fished out a packet of cigarettes. He felt this was only the beginning of his success. Uttar Pradesh, Delhi, Agra, Allahabad, Varanasi, Lucknow—there were so many other states to visit, so many, many places to go to. A whole new world waited for him. He would travel abroad; and he would show them how a young man from Bengal could be successful anywhere in the world—even in America, the land that had produced the famous Houdini. Oh yes, he would show them all. This was just the beginning.

Anil came panting. 'Everything's fine,' he said.

'Did you check the locks?'

'Yes, sir.'

'Good.'

'I'm in the third bogey from yours.'

'Have they given the "line-clear" signal?'

'They're about to. I'll go now, sir. Would you like a cup of tea at Burdwan?'

'Yes, that would be nice.'

'I'll get it then.'

Anil left. Surapati lit his cigarette and looked out of the window absentmindedly. The sight of the jostling crowds, the porters running about and the sound of a hawker's cry soon melted away. His mind went back to his childhood. He was thirty-three now; on that particular day he could not have been more than eight. By the side of the road in the small village where he lived sat an old woman with a gunny bag in front of her, surrounded by a large crowd. How old could she have been? Sixty? Ninety? It might have been anything. Her age did not matter. What mattered was what she did with her hands. She'd take any object—a coin, a marble, a top, a betel nut, even a guava—and it would vanish before their eyes. The old woman kept up an endless patter until the lost object reappeared out of nowhere. She took a rupee from Kalu Kaka and it disappeared. Much upset, Kalu Kaka began to lose his temper. The old woman giggled and— hey presto—the rupee was there for all see. Kalu Kaka's eyes nearly popped out.

Surapati could not concentrate on anything much after that day. He never saw that old woman again. Nor did he see such a startling performance anywhere else.

He was sixteen when he came to Calcutta for further studies. The first thing he did upon arrival was to buy as many books on magic as he possibly could and to begin practising the tricks they taught. It meant standing before a mirror for hours with several packs of cards, going through the instructions step by step. But soon, he had mastered them all. Then he began performing at small get-togethers and parties given by friends.

When he was in his second year in college, one of his friends, Gautam, invited Surapati to his sister's wedding. It later proved to be the most memorable evening in the history of Surapati's training as a magician, for that day he met Tripura Babu for the first time.

A huge shamiana stood behind a house in Swinhoe Street. Tripuracharan Mallik sat under it, surrounded by a group of other wedding guests. At first glance, he seemed quite ordinary—about forty-eight years old, curly hair parted at one side, a smile on his lips and the corners of his mouth streaked with the juice of paan. A man no different from the millions one saw every day. But a closer look at what was happening on the mattress in front of him was enough for one's judgement to undergo a quick change. Surapati, at first, could not believe his own eyes. A silver coin went rolling towards a golden ring kept about a yard away. It stopped beside the ring and then both came rolling back to Tripura Babu. Even before Surapati could recover from the shock, Gaulam's uncle accidentally dropped a matchbox on the ground. All the sticks spilled out. 'Don't bother to pick them up,' said Tripura Babu, 'I'll pick them up for you.' With one sweeping movement of his hand, he placed the matchsticks in a heap on the mattress. Then, taking the empty matchbox in his left hand, he began calling, 'Come to me, my dear. Come, come, come . . . ' The sticks rose in the air one by one and slipped back into the box as though they were all his pet animals, used to obeying their master's command.

Surapati went to him straight after dinner. Tripura Babu seemed very surprised at his interest. 'I have never seen anyone interested in learning magic. Most seem happy simply to see a performance,' he said.

Surapati went to his house a couple of days later. It was, actually, much less than a house. Tripura Babu lived in a small room in an old and dilapidated boarding-house. Poverty stared out of every corner. Tripura Babu told him how he tried to make a living out of his magic shows. He charged fifty rupees per show, but did not get too many invitations. The main reason for this, Surapati soon discovered, was Tripura Babu's own lack of enthusiasm. Surapati could not imagine how anyone so talented could be so totally devoid of ambition. When he mentioned this, Tripura Babu said with a sigh, 'What would be the use of trying to do more shows? How many people would be interested? How many people appreciate the talent of a true artist? Didn't you see for yourself how everyone rushed off at that wedding the minute dinner was announced? Did anyone, with the sole exception of yourself, come back to me?'

Surapati spoke to his friends after this and arranged a few

shows. Tripura Babu agreed to teach him his art, possibly partly out of gratitude and partly out of a genuine affection for the boy. 'I do not want any payment,' he said firmly. 'I am only glad that there will be someone to take things forward after I've gone. But remember—you must be patient. Nothing can be learnt in a hurry. If you learn something well, you will know what joy there is in creation. Do not expect a lot of success or fame to come to you immediately. But I know you will do much better in life than I have done, for you have got what I haven't: ambition.'

Slightly nervous, Surapati asked, 'Will you teach me all that you know? Even the one with the coin and the ring?' Tripura Babu laughed. 'You must learn to walk step by step. Patience and diligence are the key words in this form of art. It evolved in ancient times when man's will-power and concentration were far more intense. It is not easy for modern man to get there. You don't know what an effort I had to make!'

Surapati began to go to Tripura Babu regularly. But about six months later, something happened that changed his life completely.

One day on his way to college, Surapati noticed a lot of colourful posters on the walls of Chowringhee: 'Shefallo the Great', they said. A closer look revealed that Shefallo was an Italian magician. He was coming to Calcutta, accompanied by his assistant, Madame Palarmo.

They performed at the New Empire. Surapati sat in a one-rupee seat and watched each item, absolutely entranced.

He had only read about these tricks in books. Men disappeared into a cloud of smoke before his eyes, and then reappeared from the same spiralling smoke like the djinn of Alladin. A girl was placed inside a wooden box. Shefallo sawed the box into two halves, but the girl came out smiling from another box, quite unharmed. Surapati's palms hurt from clapping that night.

He watched Shefallo carefully. He seemed as good an actor as a magician. He wore a shining black suit. In his hand was a magic wand and on his head a top hat. An endless stream of objects kept pouring out of the hat. He put his hand in it once and pulled out a rabbit by its ear. Even before the poor creature had stopped flicking its long ears, out came one pigeon after another—one, two, three, four. They began to flutter around the stage. In the meantime, Shefallo had brought out a lot of chocolates from the hat which he began to throw at the audience.

Surapati noticed one more thing. Shefallo did not stop talking for an instant while he performed. He learnt later that this was what was known as magician's patter. While the audience stayed captivated by his constant flow of words, the magician quietly performed his tricks: the sleight of hand, the little deceptions.

But Madame Palarmo was different. She did not utter a word. How, then, could she deceive everyone? Surapati later learnt the answer to this one. It was possible to show certain items on the stage where the magician's own hands had very little to do. Everything could be controlled by highly mechanized equipment, operated by men from behind a black curtain. To show a man vanish into smoke or to saw a girl in two halves were both such tricks, dependent entirely on the use of equipment. Anyone who had enough money could buy the equipment and perform on stage. But, of course, one had to know the art of presentation, too. One had to have the right flair, the right touch of glamour in the total presentation of the act. Not everyone could do that. Not everyone . . .

Surapati came out of his reverie with a start. The train had just begun to pull out of the station rather jerkily when a man opened the door of his carriage from outside and clambered in. Surapati was about to protest, saying the seats were reserved, but one look at the man's face made him stop short in amazement. Good God—it was Tripura Babu!

Tripuracharan Mallik!

There had been instances in the past when Surapati had had a similar experience. To see an acquaintance in person soon after thinking about him was something that had happened to Surapati before. But finding Tripura Babu in his carriage like this made every other incident of the past pale into insignificance.

Surapati remained speechless. Tripura Babu wiped his forehead with the edge of his dhoti, placed the bundle he was carrying on the bench opposite and sat down. Then he looked at Surapati and smiled, 'Surprised, aren't you?'

Surapati swallowed hard. 'I . . . yes, I'm surprised. In fact I wasn't sure that you were still alive!'

'Really?'

'Yes. I went to your boarding-house soon after I finished college. I found your room locked. The manager told me you had been run over by a car . . . '

Tripura Babu laughed. 'That would have been rather nice. At least I might have escaped from all my worries and anxieties.'

'Besides,' said Surapati, 'I was thinking of you a little while ago.'

'Oh yes?' a shadow passed over Tripura Babu's face. 'Were you indeed thinking of me? You mean you still do? That's amazing!'

Surapati bit his lip in embarrassment. 'Don't say that Tripura Babu! How can I forget you? Are you not my first teacher? I was thinking of our days together. This is the first time I am going out of Bengal to perform, I am now a professional magician—did you know that?'

Tripura Babu nodded. 'Yes. I know all about you. That is why I have come to see you today. You see, I have followed your career very closely for the last twelve years. When you had your show at the New Empire, I went there the very first day and sat in the last row. I saw how everyone applauded. Yes, I did feel proud of you. But . . . '

He stopped. Surapati could not find anything to say. There was very little to be said anyway. One could not blame Tripura Babu if he had ended up feeling hurt and left out. After all, had he not helped Surapati in the very beginning, Surapati could not be where he was today. But what had

Surapati done for Tripura Babu in return? Nothing. On the contrary, the memory of Tripura Babu and his early days had grown quite faint in his mind. So had the feeling of gratitude.

Tripura Babu began speaking again. 'Yes, I felt proud of you that day, seeing how successful you were. But I also felt slightly sorry. Do you know why? It was because the path you have taken is not the right path for a true magician. You may be able to provide entertainment to your audience and even impress them a good deal by using all those gadgets. But none of the success is your own. Do you remember my kind of magic?'

Surapati had not forgotten. He could also remember how Tripura Babu seemed to hesitate when it came to teaching him his best tricks. 'You need a little more time,' he would say. But the right time never came. Shefallo arrived soon afterwards and, two months later, Tripura Babu himself disappeared.

Surapati had felt both surprised and disappointed not to have found Tripura Babu where he lived. But these feelings did not last for very long. His mind was too full of Shefallo and dreams of his own future—to travel everywhere, to have shows in every place, to be a name everyone recognized, to hear only applause and praise wherever he went.

Tripura Babu was staring out of the window, preoccupied, Surapati looked at him a little more closely. He did seem to have hit upon hard times. Practically all his hair had turned grey, his skin sagged, his eyes had sunk very deep into their sockets. But had the look in them dimmed even a little? No! The look in his eyes was startlingly piercing.

He sighed, 'I know of course why you chose this path. I know you believe—and perhaps I am partly responsible for this—that simplicity itself is not often rewarded. A stage performance needs a touch of glamour and sophistication, does it not?'

Surapati did not disagree. Shefallo's performance had convinced him. Surely a bit of glamour did not do any harm. Things were different today. How much could one achieve by holding simple shows at weddings? How could one claim to be successful if one had to starve? Surapati had every respect for magic in its pure form without any trimmings. But that kind of magic had no future. Surapati knew it and had, therefore decided to walk a different path.

He said as much to Tripura Babu, who suddenly became agitated. Sitting cross-legged on the bench, he leant forward excitedly. 'Listen, Surapati,' he said, 'if you knew what real magic was, you wouldn't chase what is fake. Magic is not just a sleight of hand, although even that requires years of careful practice. There is so much more to it! Hypnotism! Just think of it—you can control a person completely simply by looking at him. Then there is clairvoyance, telepathy and thought-reading. You can step into someone else's thoughts if you so wish. You can tell what a person is thinking just by feeling his pulse. If you can master this art, you need not even touch a person. All you need to do is just stare at him for a minute and you can read his thoughts. This is the greatest magic of all. Equipment and gadgets have no place in this. What is required is dedication, diligence and intense concentration.'

Tripura Babu stopped for breath. Then he slid closer to Surapati and went on, 'I wanted to teach you all this. But you couldn't wait. A fraud from abroad turned your head. You left the right path and went astray, only to make a fast buck in a world of pomp and show.'

Surapati remained silent. He could not deny any of this.

Tripura Babu seemed to relent a little. He laid a hand on Surapati's shoulder and continued in a milder tone, 'I have come today only to make a request. You may have guessed by now that my financial condition is not a sound one. I know a lot of tricks, but I haven't yet learnt the trick of making money. I know the only reason for this is my lack of ambition. Today I am almost desperate, Surapati. I do not have the strength any more to try to make my own living. All I am sure of is that you will help me, even if it means making a sacrifice. Do this for me, Surapati, and I promise not to bother you any more.'

Surapati was puzzled. What kind of help did the man want?

Tripura Babu went on, 'What I am going to tell you now may strike you as impertinent. But there is no other way. You see, it is not just money that I want. I have got a strange desire in my old age. I want to perform on a stage before a large audience. I want to show them the best trick I know. This may be the first and the last time, but I cannot put the thought out of my mind.'

A cold hand clutched at Surapati's heart. Tripura Babu finally came to the point. 'You are going to perform in Lucknow, aren't you? Suppose you fell ill at the last moment? You cannot, obviously, disappoint your audience. Suppose someone else look your place . . . ?'

Surapati felt completely taken aback. What on earth was he saying? He really must be desperate, or he wouldn't come up with such a bizarre proposal.

His eyes fixed on Surapati, Tripura Babu said, 'All you need to do is tell people you cannot perform due to an unavoidable reason, but that your place would be taken by your guru. Would people be very sorry and heartbroken? I don't think so. I do believe they'd enjoy my show. But even so, I propose you take half of the proceeds of the first evening. I would be quite happy with the rest. After that you can go your own way. I will never disturb you again. But you must give me this opportunity Surapati—just this once!'

'Impossible!' Surapati grew angry. 'What you're suggesting is quite impossible. You don't know what you're saying. This is the first time I'm going to perform outside Bengal. Can't you how see much this show in Lucknow means to me? Do you really expect me to begin my new career with a lie? How could you even think of it?'

Tripura Babu gave him a cool and level look. Then his voice cut across the railway carriage, rising clearly above all the noise, 'Are you still interested in that old trick with the coin and ring?'

Surapati started. But the look in Tripura Babu's eyes did not change.

'Why?' Surapati asked.

Tripura Babu smiled faintly, 'If you accept my proposal I will teach you the trick. If you don't ...'

His voice was drowned at this moment in the loud whistle of a Howrah-bound train that passed theirs. Its flashing light caught the strange brilliance in his eyes.

'And if I don't?' Surapati asked softly once the noise had died down.

'You will regret it. There is something you ought to know. If I happen to be present among the audience, I do have the power to cause a magician—any magician—a lot of embarrassment. I can even make him completely helpless.'

Tripura Babu took out a pack of cards from his pocket. 'Let's see how good you are. Can you take this knave from the back and bring it forward to rest on this three of clubs, in just one movement of your hand?'

This was one of the first things Surapati had learnt. At the age of sixteen it had taken him seven days to master this one. And today?

Surapati took the pack of cards and realized that his fingers were beginning to feel numb. Then the numbness spread to his wrist, his elbow and, finally, the whole arm became paralysed. In a daze, Surapati looked at Tripura Babu. His mouth was twisted in a queer smile and his eyes stared straight into Surapati's. The look in them was almost inhuman. Little beads of perspiration broke out on Surapati's forehead. His whole body began to tremble.

'Do you now believe in my power?'

The pack of cards fell from Surapati's hand. Tripura Babu picked it up neatly and said, 'Would you now agree to my proposal?'

Surapati began to feel a little better. The numbness was passing. 'Will you really teach me that old trick?' he asked wearily.

Tripura Babu raised a finger, 'Your guru, Mr Tripuracharan Mallik, shall perform in your place in Lucknow because of your sudden illness. Is that right?'

'Yes.'

'You will give me half of your earnings that evening. Right?'

'Right.'

'Well, then . . . '

Surapati fished out a fifty-paise coin from his pocket and look off his coral ring. Wordlessly, he handed them over to Tripura Babu.

*

When the train stopped at Burdwan, Anil appeared with a cup of tea and found his boss fast asleep.

'Sir!' said Anil after a few seconds of hesitation. Surapati woke instantly.

'Who . . . what is it?'

'Your tea, sir. Sorry I disturbed you.'

'But . . . ?' Surapati looked around wildly.

'What's the matter?'

'Tripura Babu? Where is he?'

'Tripura Babu?' Anil sounded perplexed.

'Oh, no, no. He was run over, wasn't he? Way back in 1951. But where is my ring?'

'Which one, sir? The one with the coral is on your finger!'

'Yes, yes, of course. And . . .'

Surapati put his hand in his pocket and took out a coin. Anil noticed that his employer's hands were trembling visibly. 'Anil,' Surapati called, 'come in quickly. Shut the windows. Okay. Now watch this.'

Surapati placed the ring at one end of the bench and the coin at the other. 'Help me God!' he prayed silently and turned a deep hypnotic stare fully on the coin, just as he had been taught a few minutes ago. The coin began rolling towards the ring and then both coin and ring rolled back to Surapati like a couple of obedient children.

Anil would have dropped the cup on the floor he was carrying if Surapati had not stretched out a hand miraculously at the last moment and caught it in mid-air.

Surapati began his show in Lucknow by paying tribute to Tripuracharan Mallik, his guru, who was no more.

The last item he presented that evening was introduced as true Indian magic—the trick of the coin and the ring.

Translated by Gopa Majumdar

Anath Babu's Terror

I met Anath Babu on a train to Raghunathpur, where I was going on a holiday. I worked for one of the dailies in Calcutta. The pressure of work over the last few months had been killing. I definitely needed a break. Besides, writing being my hobby, I had ideas for a couple of short stories that needed further thought. And I needed peace and quiet to think. So I applied for ten days' leave and left with a packet of writing paper in my suitcase.

There was a reason for choosing Raghunathpur. An old college mate of mine, Biren Biswas, had his ancestral home there. We were chatting in the Coffee House one evening, talking of possible places where one might spend one's holiday. When he heard that I had applied for leave, Biren promptly offered me free accommodation in Raghunathpur. 'I would have gone with you,' he said, 'but you know how tied up I am at the moment. You won't have any problem, though. Bharadwaj will look after you. He's worked for our family for fifty years.'

Our coach was packed. Anathbandhu Mitra happened to be sitting right next to me. He was around fifty, not very tall, hair parted in the middle, a sharp look in his eyes and an amused smile playing on his lips. But his clothes! He appeared to have dressed for a role in a play set fifty years ago. Nobody these days wore a jacket like that, or such collars, glasses or boots.

We began to chat. It turned out that he, too, was going to Raghunathpur. 'Are you also going on a holiday?' I asked him. But he did not answer and seemed to grow a little pensive. Or it may be that he had failed to hear my question in the racket that the train was making.

The sight of Biren's house pleased me very much. It was a nice house, with a strip of land in front that had both vegetables and flowers growing in it. There were no other houses nearby, so the possibility of being disturbed by the neighbours was non-existent.

Despite protests from Bharadwaj, I chose the room in the attic for myself. It was an airy little room, very comfortable and totally private. I moved my things upstairs and began to unpack. It was then that I realized I had left my razor blades behind. 'Never mind,' said Bharadwaj, 'Kundu

Babu's shop is only a five-minute walk from here. You'll get your bilades there.'

I left for the shop soon after tea, at around 4 p.m. It appeared that the place was used more or less like a club. About seven middle-aged men were seated inside on wooden benches, chatting away merrily. One of them was saying rather agitatedly, 'Well, it's not something I have only heard about. I saw the whole thing with my own eyes. All right, so it happened thirty years ago. But that kind of thing cannot get wiped out from one's memory, can it? I shall never forget what happened, especially since Haladhar Datta was a close friend of mine. In fact, even now I can't help feeling partly responsible for his death.'

I bought a packet of 7 O'Clock blades. Then I began to loiter, looking at things I didn't really need. The gentleman continued, 'Just imagine, my own friend laid a bet with me for just ten rupees and went to spend a night in that west room. I waited for a long time the next morning for him to turn up but when he didn't, I went with Jiten Bakshi, Haricharan Saha and a few others to look for him in the Haldar mansion. And we found him in the same room— lying dead on the floor, stone cold, eyes open and staring at the ceiling. The naked fear I saw in those eyes could only mean one thing, I tell you: ghosts. There was no injury on his person, no sign of snake-bite or anything like that. So what else could have killed him but a ghost? You tell me?'

Another five minutes in the shop gave me a rough idea of what they were talking about. There was, apparently, a two-hundred-year-old mansion in the southern corner of Raghunathpur, which had once been owned by the Haldars, the local zamindars. It had lain abandoned for years. A particular room in this mansion that faced the west was supposed to be haunted. Although in the last thirty years no one had dared to spend a night in it after the death of Haladhar Datta, the residents of Raghunathpur still felt a certain thrill thinking of the unhappy spirit that haunted the room. The reason behind this belief was both the mysterious death of Haladhar Datta, and the many instances of murders and suicides in the history of the Haldar family.

Intrigued by this conversation, I came out of the shop to find Anathbandhu Mitra, the gentleman I had met on the train, standing outside, a smile on his lips.

'Did you hear what they were saying?' he asked.

'Yes, I couldn't help it.'

'Do you believe in it?'

'In what? Ghosts?'

'Yes.'

'Well, you see, I have heard of haunted houses often enough. But never have I met anyone who has actually stayed in one and seen anything. So I don't quite . . .'

Anath Babu's smile deepened.

'Would you like to see it?' he said.

'What?'

'That house.'

'See? How do you mean?'

'Only from the outside. It's not very far from here. One

mile, at the most. If you go straight down this road, past the twin temples and then turn right, it's only a quarter of a mile from there.'

The man seemed quite interesting. Besides, there was no need to return home quite so soon. So I went with him.

*

The Haldar mansion was not easily visible. Most of it was covered by a thick growth of wild plants and creepers. Only the top of the gate that towered above everything else was visible a good ten minutes before one reached the house. The gate was really huge. The nahabatkhana over it was a shambles. A long drive led to the front veranda. A couple of statues and the remains of a fountain told us that there used to be a garden in the space between the house and the gate. The house was strangely structured. There was absolutely nothing in it that could have met even the lowest of aesthetic standards. The whole thing seemed only a shapeless heap. The last rays of the setting sun fell across the mossy walls.

Anath Babu stared at it for a minute. Then he said, 'As far as I know, ghosts and spirits don't come out in daylight. Why don't we,' he added, winking, 'go and take a look at that room?'

'That west room? The one . . .?'

'Yes. The one in which Haladhar Datta died.'

The man's interest in the matter seemed a bit exaggerated. Anath Babu read my mind.

'I can see you're surprised. Well, I don't mind telling you the truth. The only reason behind my arrival in Raghunathpur is this house.'

'Really?'

'Yes. In Calcutta I had heard that the house was haunted. I came all the way to see if I could catch a glimpse of the ghost. You asked me on the train why I was coming here. I didn't reply, which must have appeared rude. But I had decided to wait until I got to know you a little better before telling you.'

'But why did you have to come all the way from Calcutta to chase a ghost?'

'I'll explain that in a minute. I haven't yet told you about my profession, have I? The fact is that I am an authority on ghosts and all things supernatural. I have spent the last twenty-five years doing research in this area. I have read everything that's ever been published on life after death, spirits that haunt the earth, vampires, werewolves, black magic, voodoo—the lot. I had to learn seven different languages to do this. There is a Professor Norton in London who has a similar interest. I have been in correspondence with him over the last three years. My articles have been published in well-known magazines in Britain. I don't wish to sound boastful, but I think it would be fair to say that no one in this country has as much knowledge about these things as I do.'

He spoke very sincerely. The thought that he might be telling lies or exaggerating did not cross my mind at all. On the contrary, I found it quite easy to believe what he told me and even felt some respect for the man.

After a few moments of silence, he said, 'I have stayed in at least three hundred haunted houses all over the country.'

'Goodness!'

'Yes. In places like Jabalpur, Cherrapunji, Kanthi, Katoa, Jodhpur, Azimganj, Hazaribagh, Shiuri, Barasat . . . and so many others. I've stayed in fifty-six dak bungalows, and at least thirty indigo cottages. Besides these, there are about fifty haunted houses in Calcutta and its suburbs where I've spent my nights. But . . .'

Anath Babu stopped. Then he shook his head and said, 'The ghosts have eluded me. Perhaps they like to visit only those who don't want to have anything to do with them. I have been disappointed time and again. Only once did I feel the presence of something strange in an old building in Tiruchirapalli near Madras. It used to be a club during British times. Do you know what happened? The room was dark and there was no breeze at all. Yet, each time I tried to light a candle, someone—or something—kept snuffing it out. I had to waste twelve matchsticks. However, with the thirteenth I did manage to light the candle but, as soon as it was lit, the spirit vanished. Once, in a house in Calcutta, too, I had a rather interesting experience. I was sitting in a dark room as usual, waiting for something to happen, when I suddenly felt a mosquito bite my scalp! Quite taken aback, I felt my head and discovered that every single strand of my hair had disappeared. I was totally bald! Was it really my own head? Or had I touched someone else's? But no, the mosquito bite was real enough. I switched on my torch quickly and peered into the mirror. All my hair was intact. There was no sign of baldness.

'These were the only two ghostly experiences I've had in all these years. I had given up all hope of finding anything anywhere. But, recently, I happened to read in an old magazine about this house in Raghunathpur. So I thought I'd come and try my luck for the last time.'

We had reached the front door. Anath Babu looked at his watch and said, 'The sun sets today at 5.31 p.m. It's now 5.15. Let's go and take a quick look before it gets dark.'

Perhaps his interest in the supernatural was contagious. I readily accepted his proposal. Like him, I felt eager to see the inside of the house and that room in particular.

We walked in through the front door. There was a huge courtyard and something that looked like a stage. It must have been used for pujas and other festivals. There was no sign now of the joy and laughter it must once have witnessed.

There were verandas around the courtyard. To our right lay a broken palanquin, and beyond it was a staircase going up.

It was so dark on the staircase that Anath Babu had to take a torch out of his pocket and switch it on. We had to demolish an invisible wall of cobwebs to make our way. When we finally reached the first floor, I thought to myself, 'It wouldn't be surprising at all if this house did turn out to be haunted.'

We stood in the passage and made some rough calculations. The room on our left must be the famous west room, we decided. Anath Babu said, 'Let's not waste any time. Come with me.'

There was only one thing in the passage—a grandfather clock. Its glass was broken, one of its hands was missing and the pendulum lay to one side.

The door to the west room was closed. Anath Babu pushed it gently with his forefinger. A nameless fear gave me goosepimples. The door swung open.

But the room revealed nothing unusual. It may have been a living room once. There was a big table in the middle with a missing top. Only the four legs stood upright. An easy chair stood near the window, although sitting in it now would not be very easy as it had lost one of its arms and a portion of its seat.

I glanced up and saw that bits and pieces of an old-fashioned, hand-pulled fan still hung from the ceiling. It didn't have a rope, the wooden bar was broken and its main body torn.

Apart from these objects, the room had a shelf that must once have held rifles, a pipeless hookah, and two ordinary chairs, also with broken arms.

Anath Babu appeared to be deep in thought. After a while, he said, 'Can you smell something?'

'Smell what?'

'Incense, oil and burning flesh . . . all mixed together . . .' I inhaled deeply, but could smell nothing beyond the usual musty smell that comes from a room that has been kept shut for a long time.

So I said, 'Why, no, I don't think I can . . . '

Anath Babu did not say anything. Then, suddenly, he struck his left hand with his right and exclaimed, 'God! I know this smell well! There is bound to be a spirit lurking about in this house, though whether or not he'll make an appearance remains to be seen. Let's go!'

Anath Babu decided to spend the following night in the Haldar mansion. On our way back, he said, 'I won't go tonight because tomorrow is a moonless night, the most appropriate time for ghosts and spirits to come out. Besides, I need a few things which I haven't got with me today. I'll bring those tomorrow. Today I had come only to make a survey.'

Before we parted company near Biren's house, he lowered his voice and said, 'Please don't tell anyone else about my plan. From what I heard today, people here are so superstitious and easily frightened that they might actually try to stop me from going in if they came to know of my plan. And,' he added, 'please don't mind that I didn't ask you to join me. One has to be alone, you see, for something like this . . . '

*

I sat down the next day to write, but could not concentrate. My mind kept going back to the west room in that mansion. God knew what kind of experience awaited Anath Babu. I could not help feeling a little restless and anxious.

I accompanied Anath Babu in the evening, right up to the gate of the Haldar mansion. He was wearing a black high-necked jacket today. From his shoulder hung a flask and in his hand he carried the same torch he had used the day before. He took out a couple of small bottles from his pocket before going into the house. 'Look,' he said, 'this one has a special oil, made with my own formula. It is an excellent mosquito repellent. And this one here has carbolic acid in it. If I spread it in and around the room, I'll be safe from snakes.'

He put the bottles back in his pocket, raised the torch and touched his head with it. Then he waved me a final salute and walked in, his heavy boots clicking on the gravel.

I could not sleep well that night. As soon as dawn broke, I told Bharadwaj to fill a thermos flask with enough tea for two. When the flask arrived, I left once more for the Haldar mansion.

No one was about. Should I call out to Anath Babu, or should I go straight up to the west room? As I stood debating, a voice said, 'Here—this way!'

Anath Babu was coming out of the little jungle of wild plants from the eastern side of the house, a neem twig in his hand. He certainly did not look like a man who might have had an unnatural or horrific experience the night before.

He grinned broadly as he came closer.

'I had to search for about half an hour before I could find a neem tree. I prefer this to a toothbrush, you see.'

I felt hesitant to ask him about the previous night.

'I brought some tea,' I said instead. 'Would you like some here, or would you rather go home?'

'Oh, come along. Let's sit by that fountain.'

Anath Babu took a long sip of his tea and said, 'Aaah!' with great relish. Then he turned to me and said with a twinkle in his eye, 'You're dying to know what happened, aren't you?'

'Yes, I mean . . . yes, a little . . .'

'All right. I will tell you everything. But let me just say this one thing right away—the whole expedition was highly successful!'

He poured himself a second mug of tea and began his tale:

'It was 5 p.m. when you left me here. I looked around for a bit before going into the house. One has to be careful, you know. There are times when animals and other living beings can cause more harm than ghosts. But I didn't find anything dangerous. Then I went in and looked into the rooms in the ground floor that were open. None had any furniture left. All I could find was some old rubbish in one and a few bats hanging from the ceiling in another. They didn't budge as I went in, so I came out again without disturbing them.

'I went upstairs at around 6.30 p.m. and began making preparations for the night. I had taken a duster with me. The first thing I did was to dust that easy chair. Heaven knows how long it had lain there.

'The room felt stuffy, so I opened the window. The door to the passage was also left open, just in case Mr Ghost wished to make his entry through it. Then I placed the flask and the torch on the floor and lay down on the easy chair. It was quite uncomfortable but, having spent many a night before under far more weird circumstances, I did not mind.

'The sun had set at 5.30. It grew dark quite soon. And that smell grew stronger. I don't usually get worked up, but I must admit last night I felt a strange excitement.

'I couldn't tell you the exact time, but I guess it must have been around 9 p.m. when a firefly flew in through the window and buzzed around the room for a minute before flying out.

'Gradually, the jackals in the distance stopped their chorus, and the crickets fell silent. I cannot tell when I fell asleep.

'I was awoken by a noise. It was the noise of a clock striking midnight. A deep, yet melodious chime came from the passage. Now fully awake, I noticed two other things—first, I was lying quite comfortably in the easy chair. The torn portion wasn't torn any more, and someone had tucked a cushion behind my back. Secondly, a brand new fan hung over my head; a long rope from it went out to the passage and an unseen hand was pulling it gently.

'I was staring at these things and enjoying them thoroughly, when I realized that from somewhere in the moonless night a full moon had appeared. The room was flooded with bright moonlight. Then the aroma of something totally unexpected hit my nostrils. I turned and found a hookah by my side, the rich smell of the best quality tobacco filling the room.'

Anath Babu stopped. Then he smiled and said, 'Quite a pleasant situation, wouldn't you agree?'

I said, 'Yes, indeed. So you spent the rest of the night pretty comfortably, did you?'

At this, Anath Babu suddenly grew grave and sank into a deep silence. I waited for him to resume speaking, but when he didn't, I turned impatient. 'Do you mean to say,' I asked, 'that you really didn't have any reason to feel frightened? You didn't see a ghost, after all?'

Anath Babu looked at me. But there was not even the slightest trace of a smile on his lips. His voice sounded hoarse as he asked, 'When you went into the room the day before yesterday, did you happen to look carefully at the ceiling?'

'No, I don't think I did. Why?'

'There is something rather special about it. I cannot tell you the rest of my story without showing it to you. Come, let's go in.'

We began climbing the dark staircase again. On our way to the first floor, Anath Babu said only one thing: 'I will not have to chase ghosts again, Sitesh Babu. Never. I have finished with them.'

I looked at the grandfather clock in the passage. It stood just as it had done two days ago.

We stopped in front of the west room. 'Go in,' said Anath Babu.

The door was closed. I pushed it open and went in. Then my eyes fell on the floor, and a wave of horror swept over me.

Who was lying on the floor, heavy boots on his feet? And whose laughter was that, loud and raucous, coming from the passage outside, echoing through every corner of the Haldar mansion? Drowning me in it, paralysing my senses, my mind . . . ? Could it be . . . ? I could think no more.

When I opened my eyes, I found Bharadwaj standing at the foot of my bed, and Bhabatosh Majumdar fanning me furiously. 'Oh, thank goodness you've come around!' he exclaimed. 'If Sidhucharan hadn't seen you go into that house, heaven knows what might have happened. Why on earth did you go there, anyway?'

I could only mutter faintly, 'Last night, Anath Babu . . . '

Bhabatosh Babu cut me short, 'Anath Babu! It's too late now to do anything about him. Obviously, he didn't believe a word of what I had said the other day. Thank God you didn't go with him to spend the night in that room. You saw what happened to him, didn't you? Exactly the same thing had happened to Haladhar Datta all those years ago. Lying on the floor, cold and stiff, the same look of horror in his open eyes, staring at the ceiling.'

I thought quietly to myself, 'No, he's not lying there cold and stiff. I know what's become of Anath Babu after his death. I might find him, even tomorrow morning, perhaps, if I bothered to go back. There he would be wearing a black jacket and heavy boots, coming out of the jungle in the Haldar mansion, a neem twig in his hand, grinning from ear to ear.'

Translated by Gopa Majumdar

Shibu and the Monster

'Hey—Shibu! Come here!'
Shibu was often hailed thus by Phatikda on his way to school. Phatikda alias Loony Phatik.

He lived in a small house with a tin roof, just off the main crossing, where an old, rusted steamroller had been lying for the last ten years. Phatikda tinkered with God knew how many different things throughout the day. All Shibu knew was that he was very poor and that people said he went mad because he worked far too hard when he was a student. However, some of Phatikda's remarks made Shibu think that few people had his intelligence.

But it was indeed true that most of what he said sounded perfectly crazy.

'I say—did you notice the moon last night? The left side seemed sort of extended, as though it had grown a horn!' Or, 'All the crows seem to have caught a cold. Haven't you heard the odd way in which they're cawing?'

Shibu was mostly amused when he heard Phatikda talk like this, but at times he did get annoyed. Getting involved in a totally meaningless and irrelevant conversation was a waste of time. So he did not always stop for a chat. 'Not today, Phatikda, I shall come tomorrow,' he would say and skip along to school.

He did not really want to stop today, but Phatikda seemed more insistent than usual.

'You may come to harm if you do not listen to what I have to say.'

Shibu had heard that insane people, unlike normal people, could sometimes make accurate predictions. He certainly did not want to come to harm. So, feeling a little nervous, he began walking towards Phatikda's house.

Phatikda was pouring coconut water into a hookah. 'Have you noticed Janardan Babu?' he said.

Janardan Babu was the new maths teacher in Shibu's school. He had arrived about ten days ago.

'I see him every day,' said Shibu. 'Why—I have maths in the very first period today!'

Phatikda clicked his tongue in annoyance, 'Tch, tch. Seeing and observing are two different things, do you understand? Look, can you tell me how many little holes your belt has got? And how many buttons are there on your shirt? Try telling me without looking!'

Shibu failed to come up with the correct answers.

Phatikda said, 'See what I mean? You've obviously never noticed these things, although the shirt and the belt you're wearing are your own. Similarly, you have never noticed Janardan Babu.'

'What should I have noticed? Anything in particular?'

Phatikda began smoking his hookah. 'Yes, say, his teeth. Have you noticed them?'

'Teeth?'

'Yes, teeth.'

'How could I have noticed them? He doesn't ever smile!'

This was true. Janardan Babu was not exactly cantankerous, but no other teacher was as grave and sombre as him.

Phatikda said, 'All right. Try to notice his teeth if he does smile. And then come and tell me what you've seen.'

A strange thing happened that day. Janardan Babu laughed in Shibu's class. It happened when, referring to some geometrical designs, Janardan Babu asked what had four arms. 'Gods, sir,' Shankar cried, 'the gods in heaven have four arms!' At this Janardan Babu began chuckling noisily. Shibu's eyes went straight to his teeth.

Phatikda was crushing some object with a heavy stone crusher when Shibu reached his house that evening. He looked at Shibu and said, 'If this medicine I'm making has the desired effect, I'll be able to change colours like a chameleon.'

Shibu said, 'Phatikda, I've seen them.'

'What?'

'Teeth.'

'Oh. What did they look like?'

'They were all right, except that they were stained with paan and two of them were longer than the others.'

'Which two?'

'By the side. About here.' Shibu pointed to the sides of his mouth.

'I see. Do you know what those teeth are called?'

'What?'

'Canine teeth. Like dogs have.'

'Oh.'

'Have you ever seen any other man with such large canine teeth?'

'Perhaps not.'

'Who has such teeth?'

'Dogs?'

'Idiot! Why just dogs? All carnivorous animals have large canine teeth. They use them to tear through the flesh and bones of their prey. Especially the wild animals.'

'I see.'

'And who else has them?'

Shibu began racking his brains. Who else? Who had teeth anyway, except men and animals?

Phatikda dropped a walnut and a pinch of pepper into the mixture he was making and said, 'You don't know, do you? Why, monsters have such teeth!'

Monsters? What had monsters to do with Janardan Babu? And why talk of monsters today? They were present only in fairy tales. They had large, strong teeth and their backs were bent . . .

Shibu started.

Janardan Babu's back was definitely not straight. He stooped. Someone had mentioned that this was so because he had lumbago.

Large teeth, bent backs . . . what else did monsters have? Red eyes.

Shibu had not had the chance to notice Janardan Babu's eyes for he always wore glasses that seemed to be tinted. It was impossible to tell whether the eyes behind those were red or purple or green.

*

Shibu was good at maths. LCM, HCF, Algebra, Arithmetic—he sailed through them all. At least, he used to, until a few days ago. During the time of his old maths teacher, Pearicharan Babu, Shibu had often got full marks. But he now began to have problems, although he did try to pull himself together by constantly telling himself, 'It just cannot be. A man cannot be a monster. Not in these modern times. Janardan Babu is not a monster. He is a man.'

He was repeating these words silently in class when a disastrous thing happened.

Janardan Babu was writing something on the blackboard. Suddenly he turned around, took off his glasses and began polishing them absent-mindedly with one end of the cotton shawl he was wearing. He raised his eyes after a while and they looked straight into Shibu's. Shibu went cold with fear. The whites of Janardan Babu's eyes were not white at all. Both eyes were red. As red as a tomato. After this, Shibu got as many as three sums wrong.

Shibu seldom went home straight after school. He would first go to the grounds owned by the Mitters and play with the mimosa plants. After gently tapping each one to sleep, he would go to Saraldeeghi—the large, deep pond. There he would try playing ducks and drakes with broken pieces of earthenware. If he could make a piece skip on the water more than seven times, he would break the record Haren had set. On the other side of Saraldeeghi was a brick kiln. Hundreds of bricks stood in huge piles. Shibu usually spent about ten minutes here, doing gymnastics, and then went diagonally across the field to reach his house.

Today, the mimosa plants seemed lifeless. Why? Had someone come walking here and stepped on them? But who could it be? Not many people came here.

Shibu did not feel like staying there any longer. There was something strange in the air. A kind of premonition. It seemed to be getting dark already. And did the crows always make such a racket—or had something frightened them today?

Shibu took himself to Saraldeeghi. But, as soon as he had put his books down by the side of the pond, he changed his mind about staying. Today was not the day for playing ducks and drakes. In fact, today was not the day for staying out at all. He must get back home quickly. Or else . . . something awful might happen.

A huge fish raised its head from the water and then disappeared again with a loud splash.

Shibu picked up his books. It was very dark under the peepal tree that stood at a distance. He could see the bats hanging from it. Soon it would be time for them to start flying. Phatikda had offered to explain to him one day why bats' brains did not haemorrhage despite their hanging upside down all the time.

Shibu began walking towards his house.

He saw Janardan Babu near the brick kiln.

There was a mulberry tree about twenty yards from where the bricks lay. A couple of lambs were playing near it and Janardan Babu was watching them intently. He carried a book and an umbrella in his hand. Shibu held his breath and quickly hid behind a pile of bricks. He removed the top two in the pile and peered through the gap.

He noticed Janardan Babu raise his right hand and wipe his mouth with the back of it.

Clearly, the sight of the lambs had made his mouth water, or he would not have made such a gesture.

Then, suddenly, Janardan Babu dropped the book and the umbrella and, crouching low, picked up one of the lambs. Shibu could hear the lamb bleat loudly. He also heard Janardan Babu laugh. That was enough.

Shibu wanted to see no more. He slipped away but, in his haste to climb over the next pile of bricks, tripped and fell flat on the ground.

'Who's there?'

Shibu was going to pick himself up somehow when he found Janardan Babu coming towards him, having put the lamb back on the grass.

'Who is it? Shibram? Are you hurt? What are you doing here?' Shibu could not speak. His mouth had gone dry. But he certainly wanted to ask Janardan Babu what he was doing there. Why did he carry a lamb in his arms? Why was his mouth watering?

Janardan Babu stretched out a hand. 'Here, I'll help you up.'

But Shibu managed to get to his feet without help.

'You live nearby, don't you?'

'Yes, sir.'

'Is that red house yours?'

'Yes, sir.'

'I see.'

'Let me go, sir.'

'Goodness—is that blood?'

Shibu looked at his legs. His knee was slightly grazed and a few drops of blood was oozing from the wound. Janardan Babu was staring at the blood, his glasses glistening.

'Let me go, sir.'

Shibu picked up his books.

'Listen, Shibram.'

Janardan Babu laid a hand on Shibu's back. Shibu could hear his heart beat loudly—like a drum.

'I am glad I found you alone. There is something I wanted

to ask you. Are you finding it difficult to follow the maths lessons? Why did you get all those simple sums wrong? If you have any problem, you can come to my house after school. I will give you special coaching. It's so easy to get full marks in maths. Will you come?'

Shibu had to step back to shake off Janardan Babu's hand from his back. 'No, sir,' he gulped, 'I'll manage on my own. I'll be all right tomorrow.'

'Okay. But do tell me if there's a problem. And don't be frightened of me. What is there to be frightened of, anyway? Do you think I'm a monster that I'll eat you alive? Ha, ha, ha, ha . . . '

Shibu ran all the way to his house. He found Hiren Uncle in the living room. Hiren Uncle lived in Calcutta. He was extremely fond of fishing. Very often he came over on weekends and went fishing at Saraldeeghi with Shibu's father.

They would probably go again this time, for he saw that certain preparations had been made. But Hiren Uncle had also brought a gun. There was some talk of shooting ducks. Shibu's father could handle guns, although his aim was not as good as Hiren Uncle's.

Shibu went straight to bed after dinner. He had no doubt now that Janardan Babu was a monster. Thank God Phatikda had already warned him. If he hadn't, who knows what might have happened at the brick kiln? Shibu shivered and stared out of the window.

Everything shone in the moonlight. He had gone to bed early because he had to wake up early the next morning to study for his exams. Normally, he could not sleep with the light on. But today, if the moonlight had not been so good, he would have left the light on. He felt too frightened today to sleep alone in the dark. The others had not yet finished having dinner.

Shibu was still looking out of the window, half asleep, when the sight of a man made him sit up in terror.

The man was heading straight for his window. He stooped slightly and wore glasses. The glasses gleamed in the moonlight.

Janardan Babu!

Shibu's throat felt parched once more.

Janardan Babu tiptoed his way to the open window; Shibu clutched his pillow tight.

Janardan Babu looked around for a bit and then said somewhat hesitantly, in a strange nasal tone, 'Shibram? Are you there?'

Good God—even his voice sounded different! Did the monster in him come out so openly at night?

He called again, 'Shibram!'

This time Shibu's mother heard him from the veranda and shouted, 'Shibu! There's someone outside calling for you. Have you gone to sleep already?'

Janardan Babu vanished from the window. A minute later, Shibu heard his voice again, 'Shibram had left his geometry book among the bricks. Since it's Sunday tomorrow, I thought I'd come and return it right away. He may need it . . .'

Then he lowered his voice and Shibu failed to catch what he said. But, after a while, he heard his father say, 'Yes, if you say so. I'll send him over to your house. Yes, from tomorrow.'

Shibu did not utter a word, but he screamed silently, 'No, no, no! I won't go, I won't! You don't know anything! He's a monster! He'll gobble me up if I go to his house!'

The next morning Shibu went straight to Phatikda's house. There was such a lot to tell.

Phatikda greeted him warmly. 'Welcome! Isn't there a cactus near your house? Can you bring me a few bits and pieces of that plant? I've thought of a new recipe.'

Shibu whispered, 'Phatikda!'

'What?'

'Remember you told me Janardan Babu was a monster . . .?'

'Who said that?'

'Why, you did!'

'Of course not. You did not notice my words, either.'

'How?'

'I said try to notice Janardan Babu's teeth. Then you came back and said he had large canine teeth. So I said I had heard monsters had similar teeth. That does not necessarily mean Janardan Babu is a monster.'

'Isn't he?'

'I did not say he was.'

'So what do I do now?'

Phatikda got up, stretched lazily and yawned. Then he said, 'Saw your uncle yesterday. Has he come fishing again?

Once a Scotsman called McCurdy killed a tiger with a fishing rod. Have you heard that story?'

Shibu grew desperate, 'Phatikda, stop talking nonsense. Janardan Babu is really a monster. I know it. I have seen and heard such a lot!'

Then he told Phatikda everything that had happened over the last two days. Phatikda grew grave as he heard the tale. In the end he said, 'Hmm. So what have you decided to do?'

'You tell me what I should do. You know so much.'

Phatikda bent his head deep in thought.

'We have got a gun in our house,' said Shibu suddenly. This annoyed Phatikda.

'Don't be silly. You can't kill a monster with a gun. The bullet would make an about turn and hit the same person who pulled the trigger.'

'Really?'

'Yes, my dear boy.'

'So what do I do?' Shibu asked again. 'What's going to happen, Phatikda? My father wants me to start from today . . .'

'Oh, shut up. You talk too much.'

After about two minutes of silence Phatikda suddenly said, 'Have to go.'

'Where?'

'To Janardan Babu's house.'

'What?'

'I must look at his horoscope. I am not sure yet. But his horoscope is bound to tell me something. And I bet he has it hidden somewhere in his house.'

'But . . .'

'Wait a minute. Listen to the plan first. We will both go in the afternoon. It's Sunday today, so the man will be at home. You will go to the back of his house and call him. Tell him you've come for your maths lesson. Then keep him there for a few minutes. Say anything you like, but don't let him go back into the house. I will try to find the horoscope in the meantime. And then you run away from one side and I from the other.'

'And then?' asked Shibu. He did not like the plan much, but Phatikda was his only hope.

'Then you'll come to my house in the evening. By then I will have seen his horoscope. If he is indeed a monster, I know what to do about it. And if he's not, there is no cause for anxiety, is there?'

Shibu turned up again at Phatikda's house soon after lunch. Phatikda came out about five minutes later and said, 'My cat has started to take snuff. There are problems everywhere!'

Shibu noticed Phatikda was carrying a pair of torn leather gloves and the bell of a bicycle. He handed the bell to Shibu and said, 'Ring this bell if you feel you're in danger. I will come and rescue you.'

Janardan Babu lived at the far end of town. He lived all alone, without even a servant. It was impossible to tell from the outside that a monster lived there.

Shibu and Phatik made their separate ways to the house.

As he began to find his way to the back of the house, Shibu's throat started to go dry again. What if, when he was supposed to call out to Janardan Babu, his voice failed him?

There was a high wall behind the house, a door in the middle of the wall, and a guava tree near the door. Several wild plants and weeds grew around the tree.

Shibu went forward slowly. He must hurry or the whole plan would get upset.

He leant against the guava tree for a bit of moral support and was about to call out to Janardan Babu when he was startled by the sound of something shuffling near his feet. Looking down, he saw a chameleon glide across the ground and disappear behind a bush. There were some white objects lying near the bush. He picked up a fallen twig and parted the bush with it to take a closer look. Oh no! The white objects were bones! But whose bones were they?

Dogs? Cats? Or lambs?

'What are you looking at, Shibram?'

The same nasal voice.

A cold shiver went down Shibu's spine. He turned around quickly and saw Janardan Babu standing at his back door, watching him with a queer look in his eyes.

'Have you lost something?'

'No, sir I . . . I . . .'

'Were you coming to see me? Why did you come to the back door? Well, do come in.'

Shibu tried retracing his steps, but discovered that one of his feet was caught in a creeper.

'I have got a cold, I'm afraid,' said Janardan Babu. 'I've had it since yesterday. I went to your house. You were sleeping.'

Shibu knew he must not run away so soon. Phatikda could not have finished his job. He might even get caught. Should he ring the bell?

No, he was not really in danger, was he? Phatikda might get annoyed if he rang it unnecessarily.

'What were you looking at so keenly?'

Shibu could not think of a suitable answer. Janardan Babu came forward.

'This place is very dirty. It's better not to come from this side. My dog brings bones from somewhere and leaves them here. I have often thought of scolding him, but I can't. You see, I'm very fond of animals . . . '

Again, he wiped his mouth with the back of his hand.

'Come on in, Shibram. We must do something about your maths.'

Shibu could not wait any longer. 'Not today, sir. I'll come back tomorrow,' he said and ran away.

He did not stop running until he came to the old and abandoned house of the Sahas, quite a long way away. Goodness—he would never forget what had happened today. He didn't know he had such a lot of courage!

But what had Phatikda learnt from the horoscope? Shibu went to his house again in the evening. Phatikda shook his head as soon as he saw Shibu.

'Problems,' he said, 'great problems.'

'Why, Phatikda? Didn't you find the horoscope?'

'Yes, I did. Your maths teacher is undoubtedly a monster. And a Pirindi monster, at that. These were full-fledged monsters 350 generations ago. But their genes were so strong that even now it's possible to find a half-monster among them. No civilized country, of course, has full monsters nowadays. You can find some in the wild parts of Africa, Brazil and Borneo. But half-monsters are in existence elsewhere in very small numbers. Janardan Babu is one of them.'

'Then where is the problem?' Shibu's voice trembled a little. If Phatikda could not help, who could?

'Didn't you tell me this morning you knew what to do?'

'There is nothing I do not know.'

'Well, then?'

Phatikda grew a little grave. Then, suddenly, he asked, 'What's inside a fish?'

Oh no, he had started talking nonsense again. Shibu nearly started weeping, 'Phatikda, we were talking about monsters. What's that got to do with fish?'

'Tell me!' Phatikda yelled.

'Intestines?' Phatikda's yell had frightened Shibu.

'No, no, you ass. With such retarded knowledge, you couldn't even put a buckle on a buck! Listen. I heard this rhyme when I was only two-and-a-half. I still remember it:

Man or animal whichever thou art

Thy life beats in thy own heart

A monster's life lies in the stomach of a fish

Cannot kill him easily, even if you wish.'

Of course! Shibu, too, had read about this in so many fairy tales. A monster's life always lay hidden inside a fish. He should have known.

'When you met him this afternoon, how did he seem?' asked Phatik.

'He said he had a cold and a slight fever.'

'Yes, it all fits in,' Phatikda's eyes began to sparkle with enthusiasm. 'It has to. His life's in danger, you see. As soon as the fish is out of water, he gets fever. Good!'

Then he came forward and clutched Shibu by the collar. 'Perhaps it's not too late. I saw your uncle go back to your house with a huge fish. I thought Janardan Monster's life might be in it. Now that you've told me about his illness I'm beginning to feel more sure. We must cut open that fish.'

'But how can we do that?'

'We can, with your help. It won't be easy, but you've got to do it. If you don't, I shudder to think what might happen to you!'

About an hour later Shibu arrived at Phatikda's house dragging the huge fish by the cord he had tied around it.

'Hope no one saw you?'

'No,' Shibu panted. 'Father was having a bath. Uncle was getting a massage and Mother was inside. It took me some time to find a cord. God—is it heavy!'

'Never mind, you'll grow muscles!'

Phatikda took the fish inside. Shibu sat marvelling at Phatikda's knowledge of things. If anyone could rescue him from the danger he was in, it was going to be Phatikda. Dear God—do let him find what he was looking for.

Ten minutes later, Phatikda came out and stretched a hand towards Shibu, 'Here. Take this. Keep it with you all the time. Put it under your pillow at night. When you go to school, keep it in your left pocket. If you hold it in your hand, the monster is totally powerless and if you crush it into a powder he'll be dead. In my view, you need not crush it because some Pirindi monsters have been known to turn into normal men at the age of fifty-four. The age of your Janardan Monster is fifty-three years, eleven months and twenty-six days.'

Shibu finally found the courage to look down at what he was holding. A small, slightly damp, white stone lay on his palm, winking in the light of the moon that had just risen.

Shibu put it in his pocket and turned to go. Phatikda called him back, 'Your hands smell fishy, wash them carefully. And pretend not to know anything about anything!'

*

The next day, Janardan Babu sneezed once just before entering class and, almost immediately, knocked his foot against the threshold and damaged his shoe. Shibu's left hand, at that precise moment, was resting in his left pocket.

After a long time, Shibu got full marks in maths that day

Translated by Gopa Majumdar

The Pterodactyl's Egg

Badan Babu had stopped going to Curzon Park after work. He used to enjoy his daily visits to the park. Every evening he would go straight from his office and spend about an hour, just resting quietly on a bench, beside the statue of Suren Banerjee. Then, when the crowds in the trams grew marginally thinner, he would catch one back to his house in Shibthakur Lane.

Now new tram lines had been laid inside the park. The noise of the traffic had ruined the atmosphere totally. There was no point in trying to catch a few quiet moments here. Yet, it was impossible to go back home straight after office, packed into a bus like sardines in a tin.

Besides, Badan Babu simply had to find some time every

day to try and enjoy the little natural beauty that was left in the city. He might be no more than an ordinary clerk, but God had given him a lively imagination. He had thought of so many different stories sitting on that bench in Curzon Park. But there had never been the time to write them down. Had he, indeed, managed to find the time, no doubt he would have made quite a name for himself.

However, not all his efforts had been wasted.

His seven-year-old son, Biltu, was an invalid. Since he was incapable of moving around, most of his time was spent listening to stories. Both his parents told him stories of all kinds—fairy tales, folk tales, funny tales and spooky tales, tales they had heard and tales they had read. In the last three years, he had been told at least a thousand stories. Badan Babu had lately been making up stories himself for his son. He usually did this sitting in Curzon Park.

Over the last few weeks, however, Biltu had made it plain that he no longer enjoyed all his stories. One look at Biltu's face was enough to see that he had been disappointed.

This did not surprise Badan Babu very much. It was not possible to think up a good plot during the day; this time was spent doing his work in the office. And now that the peace of Curzon Park had been shattered, his only chance of sitting there in the evening and doing a bit of thinking was lost forever.

He tried going to Lal Deeghi a few times. Even that did not work. The huge, monstrous communications building next to the Deeghi blocked a large portion of the sky. Badan Babu felt suffocated there.

After that even the park near Lal Deeghi was invaded by tram lines and Badan Babu was forced to look for a different spot.

Today, he had come to the riverside.

After walking along the iron railings for about a quarter of a mile on the southern side of Outram Ghat, he found an empty bench.

There was Fort William, not far away. In fact, he could see the cannon. The cannonball stood fixed at the end of an iron rod, almost like a giant lollipop.

Badan Babu recalled his schooldays. The cannon went off every day at 1 p.m., the boys came rushing out for their lunch break and the headmaster, Harinath Babu, took out his pocket watch religiously and checked the time.

The place was quiet, though not exactly deserted. A number of boats were tied nearby and one could see the boatmen talking among themselves. A grey, Japanese ship was anchored in the distance. Further down, towards Kidderpore, the skyline was crowded with masts of ships and pulleys.

This was a pleasant place.

Badan Babu sat down on the bench.

Through the smoke from the steamers he could see a bright spot in the sky. Could it be Venus?

It seemed to Badan Babu that he had not seen such a wide expanse of sky for a long time. Oh, how huge it was, how colossal! This was just what he needed for his imagination to soar.

Badan Babu took off his canvas shoes and sat cross-legged on the bench.

He was going to make up for lost time and find new plots for a number of stories today. He could see Biltu's face—happy and excited!

'Namaskar.'

Oh no! Was he going to be disturbed here too?

Badan Babu turned and found a stranger standing near the bench: a man, exceedingly thin, about fifty years old, wearing brown trousers and a jacket, a jute bag slung from one shoulder. His features were not clear in the twilight, but the look in his eyes seemed to be remarkably sharp.

A contraption hung from his chest. Two rubber tubes attached to it were plugged into the man's ears.

'Hope I'm not disturbing you,' said the newcomer with a slight smile. 'Please don't mind. I've never seen you before, so . . .'

Badan Babu felt considerably put out. Why did the man have to come and force himself on him? Now all his plans were upset. What was he going to tell poor Biltu?

'You've never seen me for the simple reason that I have never come here before,' he said. 'In a big city like this, isn't it natural that the number of people one has never seen should be more than the number of people one has?'

The newcomer ignored the sarcasm and said, 'I have been coming here every day for the last four years.'

'I see.'

'I sit here in this very spot every day. This is where I do my experiments, you know.'

Experiments? What kind of experiments could one do in this open space by the riverside? Was the man slightly mad?

But what if he was something else? He could be a hooligan, couldn't he? Or a pickpocket?

Good God—today had been pay day! Badan Babu's salary—two new, crisp hundred-rupee notes—was tied up in a handkerchief and thrust into his pocket. His wallet had fifty-five rupees and thirty-two paise.

Badan Babu rose. It was better to be safe than sorry.

'Are you leaving? So soon? Are you annoyed with me?'

'No, no.'

'Well, then? You got here just now, didn't you? Why do you want to leave so soon?'

Perhaps Badan Babu was being over-cautious. There was no need to feel so scared. After all, there were all those people in the boats, not far away.

Still Badan Babu hesitated.

'No, I must go. It's getting late.'

'Late? It's only half-past five.'

'I have to go quite far.'

'How far?'

'Right up to Bagbazar.'

'Pooh—that's not very far! It's not as though you have to go to a suburb like Serampore or Chuchrah or even Dakshineshwar!'

'Even so, it will mean spending at least forty minutes in a tram. And then it takes about ten minutes to get to my house from the tram stop.'

'Yes, there is that, of course.'

The newcomer suddenly became a little grave. Then he began muttering to himself, 'Forty plus ten. That makes fifty. I am not very used to calculating minutes and hours. My system is different . . . do sit down. Just for a bit. Please.'

Badan Babu sat down again. There was something in the man's eyes and his voice that compelled him to stay back. Was this what was known as hypnotism?

'I don't ask everyone to sit by me for a chat. But you strike me as a man different from others. You like to think. You're not bound only by monetary considerations like 99.9 per cent of people. Am I right?'

Badan Babu said hesitantly, 'Well, I don't know . . . I mean . . .'

'And you're modest! Good. I can't stand people who brag. If it was all just a question of bragging, no one would have the right to do so more than me.'

The newcomer stopped speaking. Then he took out the rubber tubes from his ears and said, 'I get worried sometimes. If I pressed the switch in the dark accidentally, all hell would break loose.'

At this point, Badan Babu could not help asking the question that was trembling on his lips.

'Is that a stethoscope? Or is it something else?'

The man ignored the question completely. How rude,

thought Badan Babu. But, before he could say anything further, the other man threw a counter question at him, in an irrelevant manner.

'Do you write?'

'Write? You mean—fiction?'

'Fiction or non-fiction, it does not matter. You see, that is something I have never been able to do. And yet, so many adventures, such a lot of experience and research . . . all this should be written and recorded for posterity.'

Experience? Research? What was the man talking about? 'How many kinds of travellers have you seen?'

His questions were really quite meaningless. How many people were lucky enough to have seen even one traveller?

Badan Babu said, 'I didn't even know travellers could be of more than one kind!'

'Why, there are at least three kinds. Anyone could tell you that! Those who travel on water, those who travel on land and those who travel in the sky. Vasco da Gama, Captain Scott and Columbus fall into the first category; and in the second are Hiuen Tsang, Mungo Park, Livingstone and even our own globetrotter, Umesh Bhattacharya.

'And in the sky—say, Professor Picquard, who climbed 50,000 feet in a balloon and that youngster, Gagarin. But all of these are ordinary travellers. The kind of traveller I am talking about doesn't move on water or land or even in the sky.'

'Where does he move then?'

'Time.'

'What?'

'He moves in time. A journey into the past. A sojourn in the future. Roaming around freely in both. I don't worry too much about the present.'

Badan Babu began to see the light. 'You're talking about H.G. Wells, aren't you? The time machine? Wasn't that a contraption like a cycle with two handles? One would take you to the past and the other to the future? Wasn't a film made on this story?'

The man laughed contemptuously.

'That? That was only a story. I am talking of real life. My own experiences. My own machine. It's a far cry from a fictitious story written by an Englishman.'

Somewhere a steamer blew its horn.

Badan Babu started and pulled his chadar closer. In just a few minutes from now, darkness would engulf everything. Only the little lights on those boats would stay visible.

In the quickly gathering dusk Badan Babu looked at the newcomer once more. The last rays of the sun shone in his eyes.

The man raised his face to the sky and, after a few moments of silence, said, 'It's all quite funny, really. Three hundred years ago, right here by this bench, a crocodile happened to be stretched in the sun. There was a crane perched on its head. A Dutch ship with huge sails stood where that small boat is now tied. A sailor came out on the deck and shot at the crocodile with a rifle. One shot was enough to kill it. The crane managed to fly away, but dropped a feather in my lap. Here it is.'

He produced a dazzling white feather from his shoulder bag and gave it to Badan Babu.

'What . . . are these reddish specks?'

Badan Babu's voice sounded hoarse.

'Drops of blood from the injured crocodile fell on the bird.'

Badan Babu returned the feather.

The light in the man's eyes had dimmed. Visibility was getting poorer by the second. There had been loose bunches of grass and leaves floating in the river. Now they were practically invisible. The water, the earth and the sky had all become hazy and indistinct.

'Can you tell what this is?'

Badan Babu took the little object in his hand—a small triangular piece, pointed at one end.

'Two thousand years ago . . . right in the middle of the river—near that floating buoy—a ship with a beautifully patterned sail was making its way to the sea. It was probably a commercial vessel, going to Bali or some such place, to look for business. Standing here with the west wind blowing, I could hear all its thirty-two oars splashing in the water.'

'You?'

'Yes, who else? I was hiding behind a banyan tree in this same spot.'

'Why were you hiding?'

'I had to. I didn't know the place was so full of unknown

dangers. History books don't often tell you these things.'

'You mean wild animals? Tigers?'

'Worse than tigers. Men. There was a barbarian, about that high,' he pointed to his waist. 'Blunt-nosed, dark as darkness. Earrings hung from his ears, a ring from his nose, his body was covered with tattoo marks. He held a bow and an arrow in his hand. The arrow had a poisonous tip.'

'Really?'

'Yes, every word I utter is the truth.'

'You saw it all yourself?'

'Listen to the rest of the story. It was the month of April. A storm had been brewing for some time. Then it started. Oh, what a storm it was, the likes of which I have never seen again! That beautiful ship disappeared amidst the roaring waves before my eyes.'

'And then?'

'One solitary figure managed to make it to the shore, riding on a broken wooden plank, dodging the hungry sharks and alligators. But as soon as he got off that plank . . . oh, my God!'

'What?'

'You should have seen what that barbarian did to him . . . but then, I didn't stay till the end. An arrow had come and hit the trunk of the banyan tree. I picked it up and pressed the switch to return to the present.'

Badan Babu did not know whether to laugh or cry. How could that little machine have such magical powers? How was it possible?

The newcomer seemed to read his mind.

'This machine here,' he said, 'has these two rubber tubes. All you need to do is put these into your ears. This switch on the right will take you to the future and the one on the left will take you to the past. The little wheel with a needle has dates and years written on it. You can fix the exact date you wish to travel to. Of course, I must admit there are times when it misses the mark by about twenty years. But that doesn't make too much difference. It's a cheap model, you see. So it's not all that accurate.'

'Cheap?' This time Badan Babu was truly surprised.

'Yes, cheap only in a financial sense. Five thousand years of scientific knowledge and expertise went into its making. People think science has progressed only in the West. And that nothing has happened in this country. I tell you, a tremendous lot has indeed happened here, but how many know about it? We were never a nation to show off our knowledge, were we? The true artist has always stayed in the background, hasn't he? Look at our history. Does anyone know the names of the painters who drew on the walls of Ajanta? Who carved the temple of Ellora out of ancient hills? Who created the Bhairavi raga? Who wrote the Vedas? The Mahabharata is said to have been written by Vyasa and the Ramayana by Valmiki. But does anyone know of those hundreds of people who worked on the original texts? Or, for that matter, of those that actually contributed to their creation? The scientists in the West have often made a name for themselves by working on complex mathematical formulae. Do you know the starting point of mathematics?'

'Starting point? What starting point?' Badan Babu did not know.

'Zero,' said the man.

'Zero?'

'Yes, zero.'

Badan Babu was taken aback. The man went on.

'One, two, three, four, five, six, seven, eight, nine, zero. These are the only digits used, aren't they? Zero, by itself, means nothing. But the minute you put it next to one, it gives you ten: one more than nine. Magic! Makes the mind boggle, it does. Yet, we have accepted it as a matter of course. All mathematical formulae are based on these nine digits and zero. Addition, subtraction, multiplication, division, fractions, decimals, algebra, arithmetic—even atoms, rockets, relativity—nothing can work without these ten numbers. And do you know where this zero came from? From India. It went to West Asia first, then to Europe and from there to the whole world. See what I mean? Do you know how the system worked before?'

Badan Babu shook his head. How very limited his own knowledge was!

'They used the Roman system,' said the newcomer. 'There were no digits. All they had were letters. One was I, two was II, three was III, but four became a combination of two letters, IV. Five was again just one letter, V. There was no logic in that system. How would you write 1962? It would simply mean writing four different digits, right? Do you know how many letters you'd need in Roman?'

'How many?'

'Seven, MCMLXII. Does that make any sense at all? If you had to write 888, you would normally need only three digits. To write that in the Roman style, you'd need a dozen. DCCCLXXXVIII. Can you imagine how long it would have taken scientists to write their huge formulae? They would have all gone prematurely grey, or—worse—totally bald! And the whole business of going to the moon would have been delayed by at least a thousand years. Just think—some unknown, anonymous man from our own country changed the whole concept of mathematics!'

He stopped for breath.

The church clock in the distance struck six.

Why did it suddenly seem brighter?

Badan Babu looked at the eastern sky and saw that the moon had risen behind the roof of the Grand Hotel.

'Things haven't changed,' the man continued. 'There are still plenty of people in our country who are quite unknown and will probably always stay that way. But their knowledge of science is no less than that of the scientists of the West. They do not often work in laboratories or need papers and books or any other paraphernalia. All they do is think and work out solutions to problems—all in their mind.'

'Are you one of those people?' asked Badan Babu softly.

'No. But I was lucky enough to meet such a man. Not here, of course. I used to travel a lot on foot when I was younger. Went often to the mountains. That is where I met this man. A remarkable character. His name was Ganitananda. But he didn't just think. He wrote things down. All his mathematical calculations were done on the stones strewn about within a radius of thirty miles from where he lived. Every stone and boulder was scribbled on with a piece of chalk. He had learnt the art of travelling in time from his guru. It was from Ganitananda that I learnt that there had once been a peak higher than the Everest by about 5,000 feet. Forty-seven thousand years ago, a devastating earthquake had made half of it go deeper into the ground. The same earthquake caused a crack in a mountain, from which appeared a waterfall. The river that is now flowing before us began its course from this waterfall.'

Strange! Oh, how strange it all was!

Badan Babu wiped his forehead with a corner of his chadar and said, 'Did you get that machine from him?'

'Yes. Well, no, he didn't actually give it to me. But he did tell me of the components that went into making it. I collected them all and made the machine myself. These tubes here are not really made of rubber. It's the bark of a tree that's found only in the hills. I didn't have to go to a shop or an artisan to get even a single part made. The whole thing is made of natural stuff. I made the markings on the dial myself. But, possibly because it's hand-made, it goes out of order sometimes. The switch meant for the future hasn't been working for sometime.'

'Have you travelled to the future?'

'Yes, once I did. But not too far. Only up to the thirtieth century.'

'What did you see?'

'There wasn't much to see. I was the only person walking along a huge road. A weird-looking vehicle appeared from somewhere and nearly ran me over. I did not try going into the future again.'

'And how far into the past have you travelled?'

'That's another catch. This machine cannot take me to the very beginning of creation.'

'Indeed?'

'Yes. I tried very hard, but the farthest I could go back to was when the reptiles had already arrived.'

Badan Babu's throat felt a little dry.

'What reptiles?' he asked. 'Snakes?'

'Oh no, no. Snakes are pretty recent.'

'Then?'

'Well, you know . . . things like the brontosaurus, tyrannosaurus—dinosaurs.'

'You mean you've been to other countries as well?'

'Ah, you're making the same mistake. Why should I have had to go to other countries? Do you think our own did not have these things?'

'Did it?'

'Of course it did! Right here. By the side of this bench.'

A cold shiver ran down Badan Babu's spine.

'The Ganga did not exist then,' said the man. 'This place was full of uneven, stony mounds and a lot of wild plants and creepers. There was a dirty pond where you can now see that jetty. I saw a will-o'-the-wisp rise over it and burn brightly, swaying from side to side. In its light, suddenly, I could see a pair of brilliant red eyes. You've seen pictures of a Chinese dragon, haven't you? This was a bit like that. I had seen its picture in a book. So I knew this was what was called a stegosaurus. It was crossing the pond, chewing on some leaves. I knew it would not attack me for it was a herbivorous animal. But, even so, I nearly froze with fear and was about to press the switch to return to the present, when I heard the flutter of wings right over my head. I looked up and saw a pterodactyl—a cross between a bird, an animal and a bat— swoop upon the stegosaurus. My eyes then fell on a large rock lying nearby and the reason for such aggression became clear. Inside a big crack in the rock lay a shiny, round, white egg. The pterodactyl's egg. Even though I was scared stiff, I couldn't resist the temptation. The two animals began fighting and I pocketed the egg . . . ha, ha, ha, ha!'

Badan Babu did not join in the laughter. Could this kind of thing really happen outside the realm of fiction?

'I would have allowed you to test my machine, but . . .'

A nerve in Badan Babu's forehead began to throb. He swallowed hard. 'But what?'

'The chances of getting a satisfactory result are very remote.'

'Wh-why?'

'But you can try your luck. At least you don't stand to lose anything.'

Badan Babu bent forward. Dear God in heaven—please don't let me be disappointed!

The man tucked the tubes into Badan Babu's ears, pressed a switch and grabbed his right wrist.

'I need to watch your pulse.'

Badan Babu whispered nervously, 'Past? Or the future?'

'The past. 6,000 BC. Shut your eyes as tightly as you can.' Badan Babu obeyed and sat in eager anticipation for nearly a whole minute with his eyes closed. Then he said, 'Why, nothing seems to be . . . happening!'

The man switched the machine off and took it back.

'The chances were one in a million.'

'Why?'

'It would have worked only if the number of hairs on your head was exactly the same as mine.'

Badan Babu felt like a deflated balloon. How sad. How very sad he had to lose such an opportunity!

The newcomer put his hand inside his bag again and brought out something else.

Everything was quite clearly visible now in the moonlight.

'May I hold it in my hand?' asked Badan Babu, unable to stop himself. The other man offered him the shiny, round object.

It was quite heavy, and its surface remarkably smooth.

'All right. Time to go now. It's getting late.'

Badan Babu returned the egg. Heaven knew what else this man had seen. 'Hope you're coming here again tomorrow,' said Badan Babu.

'Let's see. There's such an awful lot to be done. I am yet to test the validity of all that the history books talk about. First of all, I must examine how Calcutta came into being. What a hue and cry has been raised over Job Charnock . . .! Allow me to take my leave today. Goodbye!'

*

Badan Babu reached the tram stop and boarded a tram. Then he slipped his hand into his pocket.

His heart stood still.

The wallet had gone.

There was nothing he could do except make an excuse and get down from the tram immediately.

As he began walking towards his house he felt like kicking himself. 'Now I know what happened,' he thought. 'When I closed my eyes and he held my hand . . . what a fool I made of myself!'

It was past 8 p.m. by the time he reached home.

Biltu's face lit up at the sight of his father.

By then, Badan Babu had started to feel more relaxed.

'I'll tell you a good story today,' he said, unbuttoning his shirt.

'Really? You mean it? It won't be a flop like all those others . . .?'

'No, no. I really mean it.'

'What kind of story, Baba?'

'The Pterodactyl's Egg. And many more. It won't finish

in a day.' If one considered carefully, the material he had collected today to make up stories for Biltu, to bring a few moments of joy into his life, was surely worth at least fifty-five rupees and thirty-two paise?

Translated by Gopa Majumdar

The Vicious Vampire

I have always harboured an intense dislike for bats. Whenever a flittermouse flits into my room in the house in Calcutta, I feel obliged to drop everything and rush out of the room. Particularly during the summer, I am distinctly uneasy at the thought of one of those creatures knocking against the fan spinning at full speed and dropping to the ground, hurt and injured. So I run out of my room and yell at the cook, Vinod, to come and rescue me. Once, Vinod managed to kill a flittermouse with my badminton racquet. To be very honest, my dislike is often mixed with fear. The very sight of a bat puts me off. What peculiar creatures they are—neither birds nor animals, with their queer habit of hanging upside down from trees. I think that the world would have been a far better place to live in if bats did not exist.

My room in Calcutta had been invaded by flittermice so many times that I had begun to think they had a strange fondness for me. But I never thought I would find a bat hanging from the ceiling in my room in this house in Shiuri. This really was too much. I could not stay in the room unless it was removed.

My father's friend, Tinkori Kaka, had told me about this house. He was a doctor and had once practised in Shiuri. After retirement, he had moved to Calcutta, but, needless to say, he still knew a lot of people in Shiuri. So I went straight to him for advice when I discovered that I would have to spend about a week there.

'Shiuri? Why Shiuri? What do you want to do there?' he asked. I told him I was working on a research project on old terracotta temples of Bengal. It was my ultimate aim to write a book on this subject. There were so many beautiful temples strewn about the country but no one had ever written a really good book on them.

'Oh, of course! You're an artist, aren't you? So your interest lies in temples, does it? But why do you want to limit yourself just to Shiuri? There are temples everywhere—Shurul, Hetampur, Dubrajpur, Phoolbera, Beersinghpur. But, perhaps, those aren't good enough to be written about?'

Anyway, Tinkori Kaka told me about this house.

'You wouldn't mind staying in an old house, would you? A patient of mine used to live there. He's now shifted to Calcutta. But I believe there is a caretaker in Shiuri to look after the house. It's a fairly large place. I don't think you'll have any problem. And you wouldn't have to pay anything, either. I snatched this man back, so to speak, from the jaws of death as many as three times. He'd be only too pleased to have a guest of mine stay in his house for a week.'

Tinkori Kaka was right. There was no problem in getting to the house. But the minute I got off the cycle rickshaw that brought me from the station and entered my room, I saw the bat.

I called the old caretaker.

'What's your name?'

'Madhusudan.'

'I see. Well, then, Madhusudan—is Mr Bat a permanent resident of this room or has he come here today to give me a special welcome?'

Madhusudan looked at the ceiling, scratched his head and said, 'I hadn't noticed it, sir. This room usually stays locked. It was only opened today because you were coming.'

'But I cannot share a room with a bat.'

'Don't worry about it, sir. It will leave as soon as the sun goes down.'

'All right. But can't anything be done to make sure it doesn't return?'

'No, sir. It won't come back. Why should it? After all, it's not as though it's built a nest here. It must have slipped in last night somehow and couldn't get out for it can't see during the day!'

After a cup of tea, I went and occupied an old cane chair

125

on the veranda. The house was at one end of the town. On the northern side was a large mango grove. Through the trees it was possible to catch glimpses of rice fields that stretched right up to the horizon. On the western side was a bamboo grove and, beyond it, the spire of a church stood tall. This must be the famous ancient church of Shiuri.

I decided to walk round to the church in the evening. I should start working from tomorrow. In and around twenty-five miles of Shiuri at least thirty terracotta temples could be found. I had a camera with me and a large stock of film. Each carving on the walls of these temples should be photographed. The temples might not last very much longer and once these were destroyed, Bengal would lose an important part of its heritage.

It was now 5.30 p.m. The sun disappeared behind the church. I got up, stretched and had just taken a step towards the stairs when something flew past my left ear making a swishing noise, and vanished into the mango grove.

I went into the bedroom and looked at the ceiling. The bat had gone. Thank goodness for that. At least I could work peacefully in the evening. Perhaps I should start writing about the temples I had already seen elsewhere in Burdwan, Bankura and the 24 Parganas.

As soon as darkness fell, I took out my torch and began walking towards the church. The red earth of Birbhum, the uneven terrain, the rows of palms—I loved them all. This was my first visit to Shiuri—I was not really here to look at nature and its beauty, yet the church and its surroundings struck me as beautiful. I passed the church and began walking further west. Then I saw what looked like a park. There was an open space surrounded by a railing. It had an iron gate.

As I came closer, I realized it was not a park but a graveyard. There were about thirty graves in it. A few had carved marble pillars. Others had marble slabs. All were undoubtedly quite ancient. The pillars were cracked. Little plants peeped out of some of these cracks.

The gate was open. I went in and began trying to read some of the hazy, indistinct epitaphs. All were graves of Britons, possibly those who had died in the very early stages of the Raj, as a result of some epidemic or the other.

One particular marble slab seemed to have a slightly more legible inscription. I was about to switch the torch on to read it, when I heard footsteps behind me. I turned around quickly. A short, middle-aged man was standing about ten feet away, smiling at me. He was wearing a black jacket and grey trousers. There was an old, patched up umbrella in his hand.

'You don't like bats, do you?'

I started. How did this stranger know that? The man laughed. 'You must be wondering how I found out. Very easy. When you were telling that caretaker to drive the bat away this morning, I happened to be in the vicinity.'

'Oh, I see.'

Now the man raised his hands in a namaskar.

'I am Jagdish Percival Mukherjee. My family has lived in Shiuri for a long time. Four generations, you know. I like visiting the church and this graveyard in the evening. I am a Christian, you see.'

It was getting darker. I headed back to the house. The man began walking with me. He seemed a bit strange, although he appeared to be harmless enough. But his voice was funny—thin and, at the same time, harsh. In any case, I could never be comfortable with people who made such an obvious attempt to get friendly.

I tried to switch on the torch, but it did not work. Then I remembered I had meant to buy a couple of batteries at the station, and had quite forgotten to do so. How annoying! I could not see a thing. What if there were snakes?

The man said, 'Don't worry about your torch. I am used to moving in the dark. I can see quite well. Careful—there's a pothole here!' He pulled me to one side. Then he said, 'Do you know what a vampire is?'

'Yes,' I said briefly.

Who did not know about vampires? Blood-sucking bats were called vampires. They sucked the blood of animals like horses and cows. I did not know whether such bats could be found in India, but I had certainly read about them in books from abroad. And those did not just talk about bats. They even spoke of bodies of dead men that came out of graves in the middle of the night to drink the blood of people who were asleep. Such creatures were also called vampires. The story of Count Dracula was something I had read in school.

It annoyed me to think that the man had raised the subject of vampires in spite of being aware of my aversion to bats.

We both fell silent.

Then we came to the mango grove and the house could be seen quite clearly. Here he stopped abruptly and said, 'It's been a pleasure meeting you. You're going to stay here for some time, aren't you?'

'About a week.'

'Good. Then we shall certainly meet again. Usually, in the evening,' he said, pointing towards the graveyard, 'I can be found there. My forefathers were buried in the same place. I shall show you their graves tomorrow.'

I said silently to myself, 'The less I see of you the better.' Bats I could not bear to look at, anyway. A discussion on those stupid creatures was even worse. There were plenty of other things to think about.

As I climbed up the steps of the veranda, I turned back for a moment and saw the man disappear among the mango trees. By that time, the jackals had started their chorus beyond the rice fields.

It was the month of October; yet, it felt hot and oppressive inside the room. I tossed and turned in my bed after dinner. I even toyed with the idea of opening the door of my room which I had closed for fear of the bat flying in again. In the end, I decided against it, not so much because of the bat, but because of something else. If the caretaker was a light sleeper, perhaps there was no danger of being burgled. But what if a stray dog came in through the open door and chewed up my slippers? This could happen easily in a small mofussil town. In fact, I had already had that kind of experience more than once. So, instead of opening the door, I opened the window that faced the west. A lovely breeze came wafting in.

I soon fell asleep and began to have a strange dream.

In my dream I saw the same man peering through the window of my room and smiling at me. His eyes were bright green and his teeth sharp and narrow. Then I saw the man take a step back, raise his arms and leap through the window. It seemed almost as though it was the sound of his arrival that woke me.

I opened my eyes and saw that dawn had broken. What an awful dream!

I rose and yelled for a cup of tea. I must finish breakfast and leave early, or I would never get all my work done.

Madhusudan seemed a little preoccupied as he placed my tea on the table in the veranda. I asked, 'What's the matter, Madhusudan? Are you unwell? Or didn't you sleep last night?'

Madhu said, 'No, babu. I am quite all right. It's my calf.'

'What happened to your calf?'

'It died last night. Got bitten by a snake probably.'

'What!'

'Yes, sir. It was only a week old. Something bit its throat—God knows if it was a cobra.'

I began to feel uneasy. Bitten on the throat? Where did I . . .? Of course. A vampire bat! Wasn't it only yesterday that I was thinking of the same thing? Vampire bats did suck blood from the throats of animals. But, of course, the calf might indeed have been bitten by a snake. That was perfectly possible, especially if the calf happened to be sleeping. Why was I trying to link the death of a calf with vampire bats?

I uttered a few words of comfort to Madhusudan and returned to my room. My eyes moved towards the ceiling involuntarily.

The bat was back.

It was my mistake. I should not have left the window open. I decided to keep all the doors and windows closed tonight, no matter how stuffy it became.

*

I spent a rather enjoyable day among the old terracotta temples. The workmanship of those who had done the carving on the walls was truly remarkable.

I took a bus from Hetampur and returned to Shiuri at about half past four in the evening.

I had to pass the graveyard in order to get home. The busy day had nearly made me forget the man I had met the day before. The sight of the man, standing under a tree just outside the graveyard, therefore, came as a surprise. Perhaps the best thing would be to pretend not to have seen him and walk on. But that was not to be. Just as I bent my head and increased the speed of my walking, he leapt towards me.

'Did you sleep well last night?'

I said 'Yes' without stopping. But it was clear that, like yesterday, he would walk with me. He began walking fast to keep pace with me. 'I have a funny habit, you see,' he said. 'I cannot sleep at night. So I sleep tight during the day and from evening to early morning, I roam around here and there. Oh, I cannot explain to you the joy of walking around at night. You have no idea how many different things are simply crying out to be seen, to be heard in this very graveyard! Have you ever thought of these beings that have spent years and years, lying under the ground, stuffed in a wooden box? Have you wondered about their unfulfilled desires? No one wants to stay a prisoner. Each one of them wants to come out! But not many know the secret of getting out. So, in their sadness, some weep, some wail and others sigh. In the middle of the night, when the jackals go to sleep and the crickets become quiet, those who have sensitive ears—like mine—can hear the soft moaning of these people, nailed into a box. But, as I told you, one would have to have very sharp ears. My eyes and ears work very well at night. Just like a bat's.'

I must ask Madhusudan about this man, I thought. There were a few questions I wanted answered, but I knew there would be no point in asking the man. How long had he really spent in Shiuri? What did he do for a living? Where did he live?

He continued to walk beside me and talk incessantly.

'I don't often make the effort to go and meet people,' he said, 'but I simply had to come and meet you. I do hope you won't deprive me of the pleasure of your company for the remainder of your stay.'

This time I could not control myself. I stopped, turned towards the man and said rather rudely, 'Look, mister, I have come only for a week. I have a vast amount of work to do. I don't see how I can possibly spend any time with you.'

The man, at first, seemed a little crestfallen at my words. Then he smiled and said in a tone that sounded mild yet oddly firm, 'You may not give me your company, but surely I can give you mine? Besides, I was not talking about the time when you'd be busy doing your work—during the day, that is.'

There was no need to waste any more time with him. I said namaskar abruptly and strode towards my house.

'Jagdish Mukherjee? I don't think . . . Oh, wait a minute! Is he short? Wears a jacket and trousers? Is a little dark?'

'Yes, yes.'

'Oh, babu, that man is crazy. Quite mad. In fact, he's only recently been discharged from the asylum. They say he's now cured. How did you come across him? I haven't seen him for ages. His father was a priest called Nilmani Mukherjee. A nice man, but I believe he, too, went quite cuckoo before his death.'

I did not pursue the matter. All I said was, 'That bat had come in again. But it was entirely my fault. I had kept the window open. I hadn't realized some of its grills were broken.'

Madhu said, 'Tomorrow morning I shall have those gaps filled. Perhaps during the night you should keep the window closed.'

After dinner, I finished writing notes on the temples I had seen that day. Then I loaded my camera with a new roll. Glancing out of the window, I saw that the clouds of last night had cleared, leaving everything awash in the moonlight.

I went and sat outside on the veranda for a while and returned to my room at around 11 p.m. Then I drank a glass of water and finally went to bed. Jagdish Mukherjee's words were still ringing in my ears. No doubt, in this scientific age, his words were no more than the ravings of a mad man. I must find out which asylum he had gone to and which doctor had treated him.

The clouds having dispersed, the oppressive feeling of the night before had gone. Keeping the window closed was not difficult. In fact, that night I had to use the extra sheet I had brought. I fell asleep soon after closing my eyes. But I woke a little while later, though I could not tell the time nor what it was that had disturbed my sleep. Then I saw a square patch of moonlight on the wall and my heart lurched.

God knew when the window had opened. Light was coming in through the open window. In that patch of light, I saw the shadow of something flying in a circle, again and again.

Holding my breath carefully, I turned my head and looked up. This time I could see the bat.

It kept flying in a circle right over my bed, and slowly began to come down.

I mustered all my courage. It would be disastrous if I lost my will power at a moment like this. Without taking my eyes off the bat, I stretched my right hand towards the bedside table and picked up my large, hardbound notebook. Just as the bat made a final swoop, ready to attack my throat, I struck its head with the notebook, using all my strength.

It went shooting out of the window, knocking once against the broken grills, and landed on the ground outside. The next instant, I thought I heard someone running across the ground.

I rushed to the window and peered out. Nothing could be seen. There was no sign of the bat.

I could not go back to sleep after that.

*

The first rays of the sun in the morning wiped out the horrors of the night. There was no reason to assume that the bat was a vampire. Yes, it had certainly come very close to me, but how could it be proved that it had done so with the intention of sucking my blood? If that weird character in the graveyard had not raised the subject of vampires, I would not even have dreamt of it. A bat in Shiuri would have struck me as no different from a bat in Calcutta.

I decided to forget the whole thing. There was some work to be done in Hetampur. I finished my cup of tea and left at around half-past six.

As I approached the graveyard, I came upon a startling sight. A few local people were carrying Jagdish Mukherjee. He appeared to be unconscious and his forehead had a large, black bruise.

'What happened to him?' I asked.

One of the men laughed.

'Fell down from a tree, probably,' he said.

'What! Why should he fall from a tree? What could he have been doing on a tree top?'

'You don't know, babu. This man is totally mad. He seemed to have made a slight recovery lately. Before that, every evening as soon as it got dark, he used to go and hang upside down from trees. Just like a bat!'

Translated by Gopa Majumdar

Patol Babu, Film Star

Patol Babu had just hung his shopping bag on his shoulder when Nishikanto Babu called from outside the main door. 'Patol, are you in?'

'Oh, yes,' said Patol Babu. 'Just a minute.'

Nishikanto Ghosh lived three houses away from Patol Babu in Nepal Bhattacharji Lane. He was a genial person.

Patol Babu came out with the bag. 'What brings you here so early in the morning?'

'Listen, what time will you be back?'

'In an hour or so. Why?'

'I hope you'll stay in after that. I met my youngest brother-in-law in Netaji Pharmacy yesterday. He is in the film business, in the production department. He said he was looking for an actor for a scene in a film they're now shooting. The way he described the character—fiftyish, short, bald-headed—it reminded me of you. So I gave him your address and asked him to get in touch with you directly. I hope you won't turn him away. They'll pay you, of course.'

Patol Babu hadn't expected such news early in the morning. That an offer to act in a film could come to a fifty-two-year-old nonentity like him was beyond his wildest dreams.

'Well, yes or no?' asked Nishikanto Babu. 'I believe you did some acting on the stage at one time?'

'That's true,' said Patol Babu. 'I really don't see why I should say no. But let's talk to your brother-in-law first and find out some details. What's his name?'

'Naresh. Naresh Dutt. He's about thirty. A strapping young fellow. He said he would be here around ten-thirty.'

In the market, Patol Babu mixed up his wife's orders and bought red chillies instead of onion seeds. And he quite forgot about the aubergines. This was not surprising. At one time Patol Babu had a real passion for the stage; in fact, it verged on obsession. In jatras, in amateur theatricals, in plays put up by the club in his neighbourhood, Patol Babu was always in demand. His name had appeared in handbills on countless occasions. Once it appeared in bold type near the top: 'Sitalakanto Ray (Patol Babu) in the role of Parasar'. Indeed, there was a time when people bought tickets especially to see him.

That was when he used to live in Kanchrapara. He had a

job in the railway factory there. In 1934, he was offered higher pay in a clerical post with Hudson and Kimberley in Calcutta, and was also lucky to find a flat in Nepal Bhattacharji Lane. He gave up his factory job and came to Calcutta with his wife. The sailing was smooth for some years, and Patol Babu was in his boss's good books. In 1943, when he was just toying with the idea of starting a club in his neighbourhood, sudden retrenchment in his office due to the war cost him his nine-year-old job.

Ever since then Patol Babu had struggled to make a living. At first he opened a variety store which he had to wind up after five years. Then he had a job in a Bengali firm which he gave up in disgust when his boss began to treat him in too high-handed a fashion. Then, for ten long years, starting as an insurance salesman, Patol Babu tried every means of earning a livelihood without ever succeeding in improving his lot. Of late he had been paying regular visits to a small establishment dealing in scrap iron where a cousin of his had promised him a job.

And acting? That had become a thing of the remote past; something which he recalled at times with a sigh. Endowed with a wonderful memory, Patol Babu would still reel off lines from some of the best parts he had played, 'Listen, O listen to the thunderous twang of the mighty bow Gandiva engaged in gory conflict, and to the angry roar of the mountainous club whizzing through the air in the hands of the great Brikodara!' It sent a shiver down his spine just to think of such lines.

Naresh Dutt turned up at half past twelve. Patol Babu had given up hope and was about to go for his bath when there was a knock on the front door.

'Come in, come in, sir!' Patol Babu almost dragged the young man in and pushed the broken-armed chair towards him. 'Do sit down.'

'No, thanks. I—er—I expect Nishikanto Babu told you about me?'

'Oh yes. I must say I was quite taken aback. After so many years . . .'

'I hope you have no objection?'

'You think I'll be all right for the part?' Patol Babu asked with great diffidence.

Naresh Dutt cast an appraising look at Patol Babu and gave a nod. 'Oh yes,' he said. 'There is no doubt about that. By the way, the shooting takes place tomorrow morning.'

'Tomorrow? Sunday?'

'Yes, and not in the studio. I'll tell you where you have to go. You know Faraday House near the crossing of Bentinck Street and Mission Row? It's a seven-storey office building. The shooting takes place outside the office in front of the entrance. We'll expect you there at eight-thirty sharp. You'll be through by midday.'

Naresh Dutt prepared to leave. 'But you haven't told me about the part,' said Patol Babu anxiously.

'Oh yes, sorry. The part is that of a—pedestrian. An absent-minded, short-tempered pedestrian. By the way, do you have a jacket which buttons up to the neck?'

'I think I do. You mean the old-fashioned kind?'

'Yes. That's what you'll wear. What colour is it?'

'Sort of nut-brown. But woollen.'

'That's all right. The story is supposed to take place in winter, so that would be just right. Tomorrow at 8.30 a.m. sharp. Faraday House.'

Patol Babu suddenly thought of a crucial question.

'I hope the part calls for some dialogue?'

'Certainly. It's a speaking part. You have acted before, haven't you?'

'Well, as a matter of fact, yes . . .'

'Fine. I wouldn't have come to you for just a walk-on part. For that we pick people from the street. Of course there's dialogue and you'll be given your lines as soon as you show up tomorrow.'

After Naresh Dutt left, Patol Babu broke the news to his wife.

'As far as I can see, the part isn't a big one. I'll be paid, of course, but that's not the main thing. The thing is— remember how I started on the stage? Remember my first part? I played a dead soldier! All I had to do was lie still on the stage with my arms and legs spread. And remember where I went from there? Remember Mr Watts shaking me by the hand? And the silver medal which the chairman of our municipality gave me? Remember? This is only the first step on the ladder, my dear! Yes—the first step that would—God willing—mark the rise to fame and fortune of your beloved husband!'

Suddenly, at the age of fifty-two, Patol Babu did a little skip. 'What are you doing?' his wife asked, aghast.

'Don't worry. Do you remember how Sisir Bhaduri used to leap about on the stage at the age of seventy? I feel as if I've been born again!'

'Counting your chickens again before they're hatched, are you? No wonder you could never make a go of it.'

'But it's the real thing this time! Go and make me a cup of tea, will you? And remind me to take some ginger juice tonight. It's very good for the throat.'

*

The clock in the Metropolitan building showed seven minutes past eight when Patol Babu reached Esplanade. It took him another ten minutes to walk to Faraday House.

There was a big crowd outside the building. Three or four cars stood on the road. There was also a bus loaded with equipment on its roof. On the edge of the pavement there was an instrument on three legs around which a bunch of people were walking about looking busy. Near the entrance stood—also on three legs—a pole which had a long arm extending from its top with what looked like a small oblong beehive suspended at the end. Surrounding these instruments was a crowd of people among which Patol Babu noticed some non-Bengalis. What they were supposed to do he couldn't tell.

But where was Naresh Dutt? He was the only one who knew him.

With a slight tremor in his heart, Patol Babu advanced towards the entrance. It was the middle of summer, and the warm jacket buttoned up to his neck felt heavy. Patol Babu could feel beads of perspiration forming around the high collar.

'This way, Atul Babu!'

Atul Babu? Patol Babu spotted Naresh Dutt standing at the entrance and gesturing towards him. He had got his name wrong. No wonder, since they had only had a brief meeting. Patol Babu walked up, put his palms together in a namaskar and said, 'I suppose you haven't yet noted down my name. Sitalakanto Ray—although people know me better by my nickname Patol. I used it on the stage too.'

'Good, good. I must say you're quite punctual.'

Patol Babu rose to his full height.

'I was with Hudson and Kimberley for nine years and wasn't late for a single day.'

'Is that so? Well, I suggest you go and wait in the shade there. We have a few things to attend to before we get going.'

'Naresh!'

Somebody standing by the three-legged instrument called out.

'Sir?'

'Is he one of our men?'

'Yes, sir. He is—er—in that shot where they bump into each other.'

'Okay. Now, clear the entrance, will you? We're about to start.'

Patol Babu withdrew and stood in the shade of a paan shop.

He had never watched a film shooting before. How hard these people worked! A youngster of twenty or so was carrying that three-legged instrument on his shoulder. Must weigh at least sixty pounds.

But what about his dialogue? There wasn't much time left, and he still didn't know what he was supposed to do or say.

Patol Babu suddenly felt a little nervous. Should he ask somebody? There was Naresh Dutt there; should he go and remind him? It didn't matter if the part was small, but, if he had to make the most of it, he had to learn his lines beforehand. How small he would feel if he muffed in the presence of so many people! The last time he acted on stage was twenty years ago.

Patol Babu was about to step forward when he was pulled up short by a voice shouting 'Silence!'

This was followed by Naresh Dutt loudly announcing with hands cupped over his mouth: 'We're about to start shooting. Everybody please stop talking. Don't move from your positions and don't crowd round the camera, please!'

Once again the voice was heard shouting 'Silence! Taking!' Now Patol Babu could see the owner of the voice. He was a stout man of medium height, and he stood by the camera. Around his neck hung something which looked like a small telescope. Was he the director? How strange!—He hadn't even bothered to find out the name of the director!

Now a series of shouts followed in quick succession—'Start sound!' 'Running!' 'Camera!' 'Rolling!' 'Action!'

Patol Babu noticed that as soon as the word 'Action' was said, a car came up from the crossing and pulled up in front of the office entrance. Then a young man in a grey suit and pink make-up shot out of the back of the car, took a few hurried steps towards the entrance and stopped abruptly. The next moment Patol Babu heard the shout 'Cut!' and immediately the hubbub from the crowd resumed.

A man standing next to Patol Babu now turned to him. 'Did you recognize the young fellow?' he asked.

'What, no,' said Patol Babu.

'Chanchal Kumar,' said he man. 'He's coming up fast. Playing the lead in four films at the moment.'

Patol Babu saw very few films, but he seemed to have heard the name Chanchal Kumar. It was probably the same boy Koti Babu was praising the other day. Nice make-up the fellow had on. If he had been wearing a Bengali dhoti and kurta instead of a suit, and given a peacock to ride on, he would make a perfect Kartik, the god considered to be the epitome of good looks. Monotosh of Kanchrapara—who was better known by his nickname Chinu—had the same kind of looks. He used to be very good at playing female parts, recalled Patol Babu.

Patol Babu now turned to his neighbour and asked in a whisper, 'Who is the director?'

The man raised his eyebrows and said, 'Why, don't you

know? He's Baren Mullick. He's had three smash hits in a row.'

Well, at least he had gathered some useful information. It wouldn't have done for him to say he didn't know if his wife had asked whose film he had acted in and with which actor.

Naresh Dutt now came up to him with tea in a small clay cup.

'Here you are, sir—the hot tea will help your throat. Your turn will come shortly.'

Patol Babu now had to come out with it.

'If you let me have my lines now . . . '

'Your lines? Come with me.'

Naresh Dutt went towards the three-legged instrument with Patol Babu at his heels.

'I say, Shoshanko.'

A young fellow in short-sleeved shirt turned towards Naresh Dutt. 'This gentleman wants his lines. Why don't you write them down on a piece of paper and give it to him? He's the one who . . . '

'I know, I know.'

Shoshanko now turned to Patol Babu.

'Come along, Dadu. I say, Jyoti, can I borrow your pen for a sec? Grandpa wants his lines written down.'

The youngster Jyoti produced a red ballpoint pen from his pocket and gave it to Shoshanko. Shoshanko tore off a page from the notebook he was carrying, scribbled something on it and handed it to Patol Babu.

Patol Babu glanced at the paper and found that a single word had been scrawled on it—'Oh!'

Patol Babu felt a sudden throbbing in his head. He wished he could take off his jacket. The heat was unbearable.

Shoshanko said, 'What's the matter, Dadu? You don't seem too pleased.'

Were these people pulling his leg? Was the whole thing a gigantic hoax? A meek, harmless man like him, and they had to drag him into the middle of the city to make a laughing stock out of him. How could anyone be so cruel?

Patol Babu said in a voice hardly audible, 'I find it rather strange.'

'Why, Dadu?'

'Just "Oh"? Is that all I have to say?'

Shoshanko's eyebrows shot up.

'What are you saying, Dadu? You think that's nothing? Why, this is a regular speaking part! A speaking part in a Baren Mullick film—do you realize what that means? Why, you're the luckiest of actors. Do you know that till now more than a hundred persons have appeared in this film who have had nothing to say? They just walked past the camera. Some didn't even walk; they just stood in one spot. There were others whose faces didn't register at all. Even today—look at all those people standing by the lamp-post; they all appear in today's scene but have nothing to say. Even our hero Chanchal Kumar has no lines to speak today. You are the only one who has—see?'

Now the young man called Jyoti came up, put his hand

on Patol Babu's shoulder and said, 'Listen, Dadu. I'll tell you what you have to do. Chanchal Kumar is a rising young executive. He is informed that an embezzlement has taken place in his office, and he comes to find out what has happened. He gets out of his car and charges across the pavement towards the entrance. Just then he collides with an absent-minded pedestrian. That's you. You're hurt in the head and say "Oh!", but Chanchal Kumar pays no attention to you and goes into the office. The fact that he ignores you reflects his extreme preoccupation—see? Just think how crucial the shot is.'

'I hope everything is clear now,' said Shoshanko. 'Now, if you just move over to where you were standing . . . the fewer people crowding around here the better. There's one more shot left before your turn comes.'

Patol Babu slowly went back to the paan shop. Standing in the shade, he glanced down at the paper in his hand, cast a quick look around to see if anyone was watching, crumpled the paper into a ball and threw it into the roadside drain.

Oh . . .

A sigh came out of the depths of his heart.

Just one word—no, not even a word; a sound—'Oh!'

The heat was stifling. The jacket seemed to weight a ton. Patol Babu couldn't keep standing in one spot any more; his legs felt heavy.

He moved up to the office beyond the paan shop and sat down on the steps. It was nearly half past nine. Every Sunday morning, devotional songs were sung in Karali Babu's house.

Patol Babu went there every week and enjoyed it. What if he were to go there now? What harm would there be? Why waste a Sunday morning in the company of these useless people, and be made to look foolish on top of that?

'Silence!'

Stuff and nonsense! To hell with your 'silence'! They had to put up this pompous show for something so trivial. Things were much better on the stage.

The stage . . . the stage . . .

A faint memory was stirring in Patol Babu's mind. Words of advice, given in a deep, mellow voice: 'Remember one thing, Patol, however small a part you're offered, never consider it beneath your dignity to accept it. As an artist your aim should be to make the most of your opportunity, and squeeze the last drop of meaning out of your lines. A play involves the work of many and it is the combined effort of many that makes a success of the play.'

It was Mr Pakrashi who gave the advice. Gogon Pakrashi, Patol Babu's mentor. A wonderful actor, without a trace of vanity in him; a saintly person, and an actor in a million.

There was something else which Mr Pakrashi used to say. 'Each word spoken in a play is like a fruit in a tree. Not everyone in the audience can reach it. But you, the actor, must know how to pluck it, get at its essence, and serve it up to the audience for their edification.'

The memory of his guru made Patol Babu bow his head in obeisance.

Was it really true that there was nothing in the part he

had been given today? He had only one word to say—'Oh!', but was that word so devoid of meaning as to be dismissed summarily?

Oh, oh, oh, oh, oh—Patol Babu uttered the word over and over again giving it a different inflection each time. After doing this for a number of times he made an astonishing discovery. The same exclamation, when spoken in different ways, carried different shades of meaning. A man when hurt said 'Oh' in one way. Despair brought forth a difficult kind of 'Oh', while sorrow provoked yet another kind. In fact, there were so many kinds of Oh's—the short Oh, the long-drawn Oh, Oh shouted and Oh whispered, the high-pitched Oh, the low-pitched Oh, the Oh starting low and ending high, and the Oh starting high and ending low . . . Strange! Patol Babu suddenly felt that he could write a whole thesis on that one monosyllabic exclamation. Why had he felt so disheartened when this single word contained a gold mine of meaning? The true actor could make a mark with this one single syllable.

'Silence!'

The director had raised his voice again. Patol Babu spotted young Jyoti clearing the crowd. There was something he had to ask him. He went quickly over to him.

'How long will it be before my turn comes, bhai?'

'Why are you so impatient, Dadu? You have to learn to be patient in this line of business. It'll be another half an hour before you're called.'

'That's all right. I'll certainly wait. I'll be in that side street across the road.'

'Okay—so long as you don't sneak off.'

'Start sound!'

Patol Babu crossed the road on tiptoe and went into the quiet little side street. It was good that he had a little time on his hands. While these people didn't seem to believe in rehearsals, he himself would rehearse his own bit. There was no one about. These were office buildings, so very few people lived here. Those who did—the shopkeepers—had all gone to watch the shooting.

Patol Babu cleared his throat and began to practise speaking this one-syllable dialogue in various ways. Along with that he tried working out how he would react to the actual collision—how his features would be twisted in pain, how he would fling out his arms, how his body would double up in pain and surprise—all these postures he performed in front of a large glass window.

Patol Babu was called in exactly after half an hour. Now he had got over his apathy completely. All he felt was keen anticipation and suppressed excitement. It was the feeling he used to have twenty years ago just before he stepped on to the stage.

The director, Baren Mullick, called Patol Babu to him. 'I hope you know what you're supposed to do?' he asked.

'Yes, sir.'

'Very good. I'll first say "Start sound". The recordists will reply by saying "Running". That's the signal for the camera to start. Then I will say "Action". That will be your cue to start walking from that pillar, and for the hero to come out of the car and make a dash for the office. You work out your steps so that the collision takes place at this spot, here. The hero ignores you and strides into the office, while you register pain by saying "Oh!", stop for a couple of seconds, then resume walking—okay?'

Patol Babu suggested a rehearsal, but Baren Mullick shook his head impatiently. 'There's a large patch of cloud approaching the sun,' he said. 'This scene must be shot in sunlight.'

'One question please.'

'Yes?'

An idea had occurred to Patol Babu while rehearsing; he now came out with it.

'Er—I was thinking—if I had a newspaper open in my hand, and if the collision took place while I had my eyes on the paper, then perhaps—'

Baren Mullick cut him short by addressing a bystander who was carrying a Bengali newspaper. 'Do you mind handing your paper to this gentleman, just for this one shot? Thanks . . . Now you take your position beside the pillar. Chanchal, are you ready?'

'Yes, sir.'

'Good. Silence!'

Baren Mullick raised his hand, then brought it down again, saying, 'Just a minute. Kesto, I think if we gave the pedestrian a moustache, it would be more interesting.'

'What kind, sir? Walrus, Ronald Colman or butterfly? I have them all ready.'

'Butterfly, butterfly—and make it snappy!'

The elderly make-up man went up to Patol Babu, took out a small grey moustache from a box, and stuck it on with sprit-gum below Patol Babu's nose.

Patol Babu said, 'I hope it won't come off at the time of the collision?'

The make-up man smiled. 'Collision?' he said. 'Even if you wrestle with Dara Singh the moustache will stay in place.'

Patol Babu took a quick glance in the mirror the man was holding. True enough, the moustache suited him very well. Patol Babu silently commended the director's judgement.

'Silence! Silence!'

The business with the moustache had provoked a wave of comments from the spectators which Baren Mullick's shout now silenced.

Patol Babu noticed that most of the bystanders' eyes were turned towards him.

'Start sound!'

Patol Babu cleared his throat. One, two, three, four, five—five steps would take him to the spot where the collision was to take place. And Chanchal Kumar would have to walk four steps. So if both were to start together, Patol Babu would have to walk a little faster than the hero, or else—

'Running!'

Patol Babu held the newspaper open in his hand. He had

worked out that when he said 'Oh!' he had to mix sixty parts of irritation with forty parts of surprise.

'Action!'

Clop, clop, clop, clop, clop—Wham!

Patol Babu saw stars before his eyes. The hero's head had banged against his forehead, and an excruciating pain robbed him of his senses for a few seconds.

But the next moment, by a supreme effort of will, Patol Babu pulled himself together, and mixing fifty parts of anguish with twenty-five of surprise and twenty-five of irritation, cried 'Oh!' Then after a brief pause, he resumed his walk.

'Cut!'

'Was that all right?' asked Patol Babu anxiously, stepping towards Baren Mullick.

'Jolly good! Why, you're quite an actor! Shoshanko, just take a look at the sky through the dark glass, will you.'

Jyoti now came up to Patol Babu and said, 'I hope Dadu wasn't hurt too badly?'

'My God!' said Chanchal Kumar, massaging his head, 'You timed it so well that I nearly passed out!'

Naresh Dutt elbowed his way through the crowd, came up to Patol Babu and said, 'Please go back to where you were standing. I'll come to you in a short while and do the needful.'

Patol Babu took his place once again by the paan shop. The cloud had just covered the sun and there was a slight chill in the air. Nevertheless, Patol Babu took off his woollen jacket and heaved a sigh of relief. A feeling of complete satisfaction swept over him.

He had done his job well. All those years of struggle hadn't blunted his sensibility. Gogon Pakrashi would have been pleased with his performance. But all the labour and imagination he had put into this one shot—did these people appreciate that? He doubted it. They probably got people off the streets, made them go through a set of motions, paid them for their labours and forgot all about it. Paid them, yes, but how much? Ten, fifteen, twenty rupees? It was true that he needed money very badly, but what was twenty rupees when measured against the intense satisfaction of a small job done with perfection and dedication?

*

Ten minutes later Naresh Dutt went looking for Patol Babu near the paan shop and found no one there. 'That's odd— the man hadn't been paid yet. What a strange fellow!'

'The sun has come out,' Baren Mullick was heard shouting. 'Silence! Silence!—Naresh, hurry up and get these people out of the way!'

Translated by Satyajit Ray

Indigo

My name is Aniruddha Bose. I am twenty-nine years old and a bachelor. For the last eight years I've been working in an advertising agency in Calcutta. With the salary I get I live in reasonable comfort in a flat in Sardar Shankar Road. The flat has two south-facing rooms and is on the ground floor. Two years ago I bought an Ambassador car which I drive myself. I do a bit of writing in my spare time. Three of my stories have been published in magazines and have been well appreciated by my acquaintances, but I know I cannot make a living by writing alone.

For the last few months I haven't been writing at all. Instead, I have read a lot about indigo plantations in Bengal and Bihar in the nineteenth century. I am something of an authority on the subject now: how the British exploited the poor peasants; how the peasants rose in revolt; and how, finally, with the invention of synthetic indigo in Germany, the cultivation of indigo was wiped out from our country— all this I know by heart. It is to describe the terrible experience which instilled in me this interest in indigo that I have taken up my pen today.

At this point I must tell you something about my past.

My father was a well-known physician in Monghyr, a town in Bihar. That is where I was born and that is where I did my schooling in a missionary school. I have a brother five years older than me. He studied medicine in England and is now attached to a hospital in a suburb of London called Golders Green. He has no plans to return to India.

My father died when I was sixteen. Soon after his death, my mother and I left Monghyr and came to Calcutta where we stayed with my maternal uncle. I went to St. Xavier's College and took my bachelor's degree. Soon after that I got my job with the advertising agency. My uncle's influence helped, but I wasn't an unworthy candidate myself. I had been a good student, I spoke English fluently, and most of all, I had the ability to carry myself well in an interview.

My early years in Monghyr had instilled certain habits in me which I have not been able to give up. One of these is an overpowering desire to go far away from the hectic life of Calcutta from time to time. I have done so several times ever since I bought my car. On weekends I have made trips to

Diamond Harbour, Port Canning, and Hassanabad along the Dum Dum Road. Each time I have gone alone because, to be quite honest, I don't really have a close friend in Calcutta. That is why Promode's letter made me so happy. Promode had been my classmate in Monghyr. After I came away to Calcutta, we continued to keep in touch for three or four years. Then, perhaps it was I who stopped writing. Suddenly the other day when I came back from work, I found a letter from Promode waiting for me on my desk. He had written from Dumka—'I have a job in the Forest Department here. I have my own quarters. Why don't you take a week's leave and come over . . .?'

Some leave was due to me, so I spoke to my boss, and on the twenty-seventh of April—I shall remember the date as long as I live—I packed my bags and set off for Dumka.

Promode hadn't suggested that I go by car; it was my idea. Dumka was 200 miles away, so it would take about five or six hours at the most. I decided to have a big breakfast, set off by ten and reach there before dusk.

At least that was the plan, but there was a snag right at the start. I had my meal and was about to put a paan into my mouth, when my father's old friend Uncle Mohit suddenly turned up. He is a grave old man whom I was meeting again after ten years. So there was no question of giving him short shrift. I had to offer him tea and listen to him chat for over an hour.

I saw Uncle Mohit off and shoved my suitcase and bedding into the back seat of my car. Just then, my ground floor neighbour Bhola Babu walked up with his four-year-old son Pintu in tow.

'Where are you off to all by yourself?' Bhola Babu asked.

When I told him, he said with some concern, 'But that's a long way. Shouldn't you have arranged for a driver?'

I said I was a very cautious driver myself, and that I had taken such care of my car that it was still as good as new— 'So there's nothing to worry about.'

Bhola Babu wished me luck and went into the house. I glanced at my wristwatch before turning the ignition key. It was ten minutes past eleven.

Although I avoided Howrah and took the Bally Bridge road, it took me an hour and a half to reach Chandernagore. Driving through dingy towns, these first thirty miles were so dreary that the fun of a car journey was quite lost. But from there on, as the car emerged into open country, the effect was magical. Where in the city did one get to see such clear blue sky free from chimney smoke, and breathe air so pure and so redolent of the smell of earth?

At about half past twelve, as I was nearing Burdwan, I began to feel the consequence of having eaten so early. Hungry, I pulled up by the station which fell on the way, went into a restaurant and had a light meal of toast, omelette and coffee. Then I resumed my journey. I still had 135 miles to go.

Twenty miles from Burdwan, there was a small town called Panagarh. There I had to leave the Grand Trunk Road and take the road to Ilambazar. From Ilambazar the road went via Suri and Massanjore to Dumka.

The military camp at Panagarh had just come into view when there was a bang from the rear of my car. I had a flat tyre.

I got down. I had a spare tyre and could easily fit it. The thought that other cars would go whizzing by, their occupants laughing at my predicament, was not a pleasant one. Nevertheless I brought out the jack from the boot and set to work.

By the time I finished putting the new tyre on, I was dripping with sweat. My watch showed half past two. It had turned muggy in the meantime. The cool breeze which was blowing even an hour ago, and was making the bamboo trees sway, had stopped. Now everything was still. As I got back into the car I noticed a blue-black patch in the west above the treetops. Cloud. Was a storm brewing up? A norwester? It was useless to speculate. I must drive faster. I helped myself to some hot tea from the flask and resumed my journey.

Before I could cross Ilambazar, I was caught in the storm. I had enjoyed such norwesters in the past, sitting in my room, and had even recited Tagore poems to myself to blend with the mood. I had no idea that driving through open country, such a norwester could strike terror into the heart. Claps of thunder always make me uncomfortable. They seem to show a nasty side of nature; a vicious assault on helpless humanity.

It seemed as if the shafts of lightning were all aimed at my poor Ambassador, and one of them was sure to find its mark sooner or later.

In this precarious state I passed Suri and was well on my way to Massanjore when there was yet another bang which no one could mistake for a thunderclap. I realized that another of my tyres had decided to call it a day.

I gave up hope. It was now pouring with rain. My watch said half past five. For the last twenty miles I had had to keep the speedometer down to fifteen, or I would have been well past Massanjore by now. Where was I? Up ahead nothing was visible through the rainswept windscreen. The wiper was on but its efforts were more frolicsome than effective. It being April, the sun should still be up, but it seemed more like late evening.

I opened the door on my right slightly and looked out. What I saw didn't suggest the presence of a town, though I could make out a couple of buildings through the trees. There was no question of getting out of the car and exploring, but one thing was clear enough: there were no shops along the road as far as the eye could see.

And I had no more spare tyres. After waiting in the car for a quarter of an hour, it struck me that no other vehicles had passed by in all this time. Was I on the right road? There had been no mistake up to Suri, but suppose I had taken a wrong turning after that? It was not impossible in the blinding rain.

But even if I had made a mistake, it was not as if I had

strayed into the jungles of Africa or South America. Wherever I was, there was no doubt that I was still in the district of Birbhum, within fifty miles of Santiniketan, and as soon as the rain stopped my troubles would be over—I might even find a repair shop within a mile or so. I pulled out a packet of Wills from my pocket and lit a cigarette. I recalled Bhola Babu's warning. He must have gone through the same trying experience, or how could he have given me such sound advice? In future—

Honk! Honk! Honk!

I turned round and saw a truck standing behind. Why was it blowing its horn? Was I standing right in the middle of the road?

The rain had let up a little. I opened the door, got out and found that it was no fault of the truck's. When my tyre burst the car had swerved at an angle and was now blocking most of the road. There was no room for the truck to pass.

'Take the car to one side, sir.'

The Sikh driver had by now come out of the truck.

'What's the matter?' he asked. 'A puncture?'

I shrugged to convey my state of helplessness. 'If you could lend a hand,' I said, 'we could move the car to one side and let you pass.'

The Sikh driver's helper came out too. The three of us pushed the car to one side of the road. Then I found out from the two men that I was indeed on the wrong road for Dumka. I had taken a wrong turning and would have to drive back three miles to get back on the right track. I also learnt that there were no repair shops nearby.

The truck went on its way. As its noise faded away, the truth struck me like a hammer blow.

I had reached a dead end.

There was no way I could reach Dumka that night, and I had no idea how and where I would spend the night.

The roadside puddles were alive with the chorus of frogs. The rain had now been reduced to a light drizzle.

I got back into the car and was about to light a second cigarette when I spotted a light through the window on my side. I opened the door again. Through the branches of a tree I saw a rectangle of orange light. A window. Just as smoke meant the presence of fire, a kerosene lamp meant the presence of a human being. There was a house nearby and there were occupants in it.

I got out of the car with my torch. The window wasn't too far away. I had to go and investigate. There was a narrow footpath branching off from the main road which seemed to go in the direction of the house with the window.

I locked the car and set off.

I made my way avoiding puddles as far as possible. As I passed a tamarind tree, the house came into view. Well, hardly a house. It was a small cottage with a corrugated tin roof. Through an open door I could see a hurricane lantern and the leg of a bed.

'Is anybody there?' I called out.

A stocky, middle-aged man with a thick moustache came

out of the room and squinted at my torch. I turned the spot away from his face.

'Where are you from, sir?' the man asked.

In a few words I described my predicament. 'Is there a place here where I can spend the night?' I asked, 'I shall pay for it, of course.'

'In the dak bungalow, you mean?'

Dak bungalow? I didn't see any dak bungalow.

But immediately, I realized my mistake. I had followed the light of the lantern, and had therefore failed to look around. Now I turned the torch to my left and immediately a large bungalow came into view. 'You mean that one?' I asked.

'Yes sir, but there is no bedding. And you can't have meals here.'

'I'm carrying my own bedding,' I said, 'I hope there's a bed there?'

'Yes sir. A charpoy.'

'And I see there's a stove lit in your room. You must be cooking your own meal?' The man broke into a smile and asked if I would care for coarse chapatis prepared by him and urad-ka-dal cooked by his wife. I said it would do very nicely. I liked all kinds of chapatis, and urad was my favourite dal.

I don't know what the bungalow was like in its heyday, but now it was hardly what one understood by a dak bungalow. Constructed during the time of the Raj, the bedroom was large and the ceiling was high. The furniture consisted of a charpoy, a table set against the wall on one side, and a chair with a broken arm. The chowkidar, or the caretaker, had in the meantime lit a lantern for me. He now put it on the table.

'What is your name?' I asked.

'Sukhanram, sir.'

'Has anybody ever lived in this bungalow or am I the first one?'

'Oh, no sir, others have come too. There was a gentleman who stayed here for two nights last winter.'

'I hope there are no ghosts here,' I said in a jocular tone.

'God forbid!' he said. 'No one has ever complained of ghosts.'

I must say I found his words reassuring. If a place is spooky, and old dak bungalows have a reputation for being so, it will be so at all times. 'When was this bungalow built?' I asked.

Sukhan began to unroll my bedding and said, 'This used to be a sahib's bungalow, sir.'

'A sahib?'

'Yes sir. An indigo planter. There used to be an indigo factory close by. Now only the chimney is standing.'

I knew indigo was cultivated in these parts at one time. I had seen ruins of indigo factories in Monghyr too in my childhood.

It was ten-thirty when I went to bed after dining on Sukhan's coarse chapatis and urad-ka-dal. I had sent a telegram to Promode from Calcutta saying that I would arrive this afternoon. He would naturally wonder what had happened. But it was useless to think of that now.

All I could do now was congratulate myself on having found a shelter, and that too without much trouble. In future I would do as Bhola Babu had advised. I had learnt a lesson, and lessons learnt the hard way are not forgotten easily.

I put the lantern in the adjoining bathroom. The little light that seeped through the door which I had kept slightly ajar was enough. Usually I find it difficult to sleep with a light on, and yet I did not extinguish the light even though what I badly needed now was sleep. I was worried about my car which I had left standing on the road, but it was certainly safer to do so in a village than in the city.

The sound of the rain drizzling had stopped. The air was now filled with the croaking of frogs and the shrill chirping of crickets. From my bed in that ancient bungalow in this remote village, the city seemed to belong to another planet. Indigo . . . I thought of the play by Dinabandhu Mitra, *Nildarpan* (The Mirror of Indigo). As a college student I had watched a performance of it in a theatre on Cornwallis Street.

I didn't know how long I had slept, when a sound suddenly awakened me. Something was scratching at the door. The door was bolted. Must be a dog or a jackal, I thought, and in a minute or so the noise stopped.

I shut my eyes in an effort to sleep, but the barking of a dog put an end to my efforts. This was not the bark of a stray village dog, but the unmistakable bay of a hound. I was familiar with it. Two houses away from us in Monghyr lived

Mr Martin. He had a hound which bayed just like this. Who on earth kept a pet hound here? I thought of opening the door to find out as the sound seemed quite near. But then I thought, why bother? It was better to get some more sleep. What time was it now? A faint moonlight came in through the window. I raised my left hand to glance at the wristwatch, and gave a start. My wristwatch was gone.

And yet, because it was an automatic watch, I always wore it to bed. Where did it disappear? And how? Were there thieves around? What will happen to my car then? I felt beside my pillow for my torch and found that was gone too. I jumped out of bed, knelt on the floor and looked underneath it. My suitcase too had disappeared.

My head started spinning. Something had do be done about it. I called out: 'Chowkidar!'

There was no answer. I went to the door and found that it was still bolted. The window had bars. So how did the thief enter?

As I was about unfasten the bolt, I glanced at my hand and experienced an odd feeling.

Had whitewash from the wall got on to my hand? Or was it white powder? Why did it look so pale? I had gone to bed wearing a vest; why then was I now wearing a long-sleeved silk shirt? I felt a throbbing in my head. I opened the door and went out on the veranda. 'Chowkidar!'

The word that came out was spoken with the unmistakable accent of an Englishman. And where was the chowkidar, and where was his little cottage? There was now a wide open field in front of the bungalow. In the distance was a building with a high chimney. The surroundings were unusually quiet. They had changed.

And so had I.

I came back into the bedroom in a sweat. My eyes had got used to the darkness. I could now clearly make out the details.

The bed was there, but it was covered with a mosquito net. I hadn't been using one. The pillow too was unlike the one I had brought with me. This one had a border with frills; mine didn't. The table and the chair stood where they did, but they had lost their aged look. The varnished wood shone even in the soft light. On the table stood not a lantern but a kerosene lamp with an ornate shade.

There were other objects in the room which gradually came into view: a pair of steel trunks in a corner, a folding bracket on the wall from which hung a coat, an unfamiliar type of headgear and a hunting crop. Below the bracket, standing against the wall, was a pair of galoshes.

I turned away from the objects and took another look at myself. Till now I had only noticed the silk shirt; now I saw the narrow trousers and the socks.

I didn't have shoes on, but saw a pair of black boots on the floor by the bed.

I passed my right hand over my face and realized that not only my complexion but my features too had changed. I didn't possess such a sharp nose, nor such thin lips or narrow chin. I felt the hair on my head and found that it was wavy and that there were sideburns which reached below my ears.

In spite of my surprise and terror, I suddenly felt a great urge to find out what I looked like. But where to find a mirror?

I strode towards the bathroom, opened the door with a sharp push and went in.

There had been nothing there but a bucket. Now I saw a metal bath tub and a mug kept on a stool beside it. The thing I was looking for was right in front of me: an oval mirror fixed to a dressing-table. I looked into it, but the person reflected in it was not me. By some devilish trick I had turned into a nineteenth-century Englishman with a sallow complexion, blond hair and light eyes from which shone a strange mixture of hardness and suffering. How old would the Englishman be? Not more than thirty, but it looked as if either illness or hard work or both had aged him prematurely.

I went closer and had a good look at 'my' face. As I looked a deep sigh rose from the depths of my heart. The voice was not mine. The sigh, too, expressed not my feelings but those of the Englishman. What followed made it clear that all my limbs were acting of their own volition. And yet it was surprising that I—Aniruddha Bose—was perfectly aware of the change in identity. But I didn't know if the change was permanent, or if there was any way to regain my lost self.

I came back to the bedroom.

Now I glanced at the table. Below the lamp was a notebook bound in leather. It was open at a blank page. Beside it was an inkwell with a quill pen dipped in it.

I walked over to the table. Some unseen force made me sit

in the chair and pick up the pen with my right hand. The hand now moved towards the left-hand page of the notebook, and the silent room was filled with the noise of a quill scratching the blank page. This is what I wrote:

27 April 1868
Those fiendish mosquitoes are singing in my ears again. So that's how the son of a mighty empire had to meet his end—at the hands of a tiny insect. What strange will of God is this? Eric has made his escape. Percy and Tony too left earlier. Perhaps I was greedier than them. So in spite of repeated attacks of malaria I couldn't resist the lure of indigo. No, not only that. One mustn't lie in one's diary. My countrymen know me only too well. I didn't lead a blameless life at home either; and they surely have not forgotten that. So I do not dare go back home. I know I will have to stay here and lay down my life on this alien soil. My place will be beside the graves of my wife Mary and my dear little son Toby. I have treated the natives here so badly that there is no one to shed a tear at my passing away. Perhaps Mirjan would miss me—my faithful trusted bearer Mirjan.

And Rex? My real worry is about Rex. Alas, faithful Rex! When I die, these people will not spare you. They will either stone you or club you to death. If only I could do something about you!

I could write no more. The hands were shaking. Not mine, the diarist's.

I put down the pen.

Then my right hand dropped and moved to the right and made for the handle of the drawer.

I opened it.

Inside there was a pincushion, a brass paperweight, a pipe and some papers.

The drawer opened a little more. A metal object glinted in the half-light.

It was a pistol, its butt inlaid with ivory.

The hand pulled out the pistol. It had stopped shaking.

A group of jackals cried out. It was as if in answer to the jackals' cry that the hound bayed again.

I left the chair and advanced towards the door. I went out into the veranda. The field in front was bathed in moonlight.

About ten yards from the veranda stood a large greyhound. He wagged his tail as he saw me.

'Rex!'

It was the same deep English voice. The echo of the call came floating back from the faraway factory and bamboo grove—Rex! Rex!Rex came up towards the veranda.

As he stepped from the grass onto the cement, my right hand rose to my waist, the pistol pointing towards the hound. Rex stopped in his tracks, his eye on the pistol. He gave a low growl. My right forefinger pressed the trigger. As the gun throbbed with a blinding flash, smoke and the smell of gunpowder filled the air.

Rex's lifeless, blood-spattered body lay partly on the veranda and partly on the grass.

The sound of the pistol had wakened the crows in the nearby trees. A hubbub now rose from the direction of the factory.

I came back into the bedroom, bolted the door and sat on the bed. The shouting drew near.

I placed the still hot muzzle of the pistol by my right ear. That is all I remember.

I woke up at the sound of knocking.

'I've brought your tea, sir.'

*

Daylight flooded in through the window. Out of sheer habit my eyes strayed to my left wrist. Thirteen minutes past six. I brought the watch closer to my eyes to read the date, April the twenty-eighth.

I now opened the door and let Sukhanram in.

'There's a car repair shop half an hour down the road, sir,' he said. 'It'll open at seven.'

'Very good,' I said, and proceeded to drink my tea. Will anyone believe me when they hear of my experience on the night of the hundredth anniversary of the death of an English indigo planter in Birbhum?

Translated by Satyajit Ray

Danger in Darjeeling

I saw Rajen Babu come to the Mall every day. He struck me as an amiable old man. All his hair had turned grey, and his face always wore a cheerful expression. He generally spent a few minutes in the corner shop that sold old Nepali and Tibetan things; then he came and sat on a bench in the Mall for about half an hour, until it started to get dark. After that he went straight home. One day, I followed him quietly to see where he lived. He turned around just as we reached his front gate and asked, 'Who are you? Why have you been following me?'

'My name is Tapesh Ranjan,' I replied quickly.

'Well then, here is a lozenge for you,' he said, offering me a lemon drop. 'Come to my house one day. I'll show you my collection of masks,' he added.

Who knew that this friendly old soul would get into such trouble? Why, he seemed totally incapable of getting involved with anything even remotely sinister!

*

Feluda snapped at me when I mentioned this. 'How can you tell just by looking at someone what he might get mixed up with?' he demanded.

This annoyed me. 'What do you know of Rajen Babu?' I said. 'He's a good man. A very kind man. He has done a lot for the poor Nepali people who live in slums. There's no reason why he should be in trouble. I know. I see him every day. You haven't seen him even once. In fact, I've hardly seen you go out at all since we came to Darjeeling.'

'All right, all right. Let's have all the details then. What would a little boy like you know of danger, anyway?'

Now, this wasn't fair. I was not a little boy any more. I was thirteen and a half. Feluda was twenty-seven.

*

To tell you the truth, I came to know about the trouble Rajen Babu was in purely by accident. I was sitting on a bench in the Mall today, waiting for the band to start playing. On my left was Tinkori Babu, reading a newspaper. He had recently arrived from Calcutta to spend the summer in Darjeeling, and had taken a room on rent in Rajen Babu's house. I was trying to lean over his shoulder and look at the sports page, when Rajen Babu arrived panting and collapsed on the empty portion of our bench, next to Tinkori Babu. He looked visibly shaken.

'What's the matter?' asked Tinkori Babu, folding his newspaper. 'Did you just run up a hill?'

'No, no,' Rajen Babu replied cautiously, wiping his face with one corner of his scarf. 'Something incredible has happened.'

I knew what 'incredible' meant. Feluda was quite partial to the word.

'What do you mean?' Tinkori Babu asked.

'Look, here it is,' Rajen Babu passed a piece of folded blue paper to Tinkori Babu. I could tell it was a letter, but made no attempt to read it when Tinkori Babu unfolded it. I looked away instead, humming under my breath to indicate a complete lack of interest in what the two old men were discussing. But I heard Tinkori Babu remark, 'You're right, it is incredible! Who could possibly write such a threatening letter to you?'

'I don't know. That's what's so puzzling. I don't remember having deliberately caused anyone any harm. As far as I know, I have no enemies.'

Tinkori Babu leant towards his neighbour. 'We'd better not talk about this in public,' he whispered. 'Let's go home.'

The two gentlemen left.

Feluda remained silent for a while after I had finished my story. Then he frowned and said, 'You mean you think we need to investigate?'

'Why, didn't you tell me you were looking for a mystery? And you said you had read so many detective novels that you could work as a sleuth yourself!'

'Yes, that's true. I could prove it, too. I didn't go to the Mall today, did I? But I could tell you which side you sat on.'

'All right, which side was it?'

'You chose a bench on the right side of the Radha restaurant, didn't you?'

'That's terrific. How did you guess?'

'The sun came out this evening. Your left cheek looks sunburnt but the right one is all right. This could happen only if you sat on that side of the Mall. That's the bit that catches the evening sunshine.'

'Incredible!'

'Yes. Anyway, I think we should go and visit Mr Rajen Majumdar.'

*

'Another seventy-seven steps.'

'And what if it's not?'

'It has to be, Feluda. I counted the last time.'

'Remember you'll get knocked on the head if you're wrong.'

'Okay, but not too hard. A sharp knock may damage my brain.'

To my amazement, seventy-seven steps later, we were still at some distance from Rajen Babu's gate. Another twenty-three brought us right up to it. Feluda hit my head lightly, and asked, 'Did you count the steps on your way back?'

'Yes.'

'That explains it. You went down the hill on your way back, you idiot. You must have taken very big steps.'

'Well . . . yes, maybe.'

'I'm sure you did. You see, young people always tend to take big, long steps when going downhill. Older people have to be more cautious, so they take smaller, measured steps.'

We went in through the gate. Feluda pressed the calling bell. Someone in the distance was listening to a radio.

'Have you decided what you're going to say to him?' I asked.

'That's my business. You, my dear, will keep your mouth shut.'

'Even if they ask me something? You mean I shouldn't even make a reply?'

'Shut up.'

A Nepali servant opened the door. 'Andar aaiye,' he said.

We stepped into the living room. Made of wood, the house had a lovely old charm. All the furniture in the room was made of cane. The walls were covered with strange masks, most showing large teeth and wearing rather unpleasant expressions. Some of them frightened me. Apart from these, the room was full of old weapons—shields and swords and daggers. Beside these hung pictures of the Buddha, painted on cloth. Heaven knew how old they were, but the golden colour that had been used had not faded at all.

We took two cane chairs. Feluda rose briefly to inspect the walls. Then he came back and said, 'All the nails are new. So Rajen Babu's passion for antiques must have developed only recently.'

Rajen Babu came into the room. Feluda sprang to his feet and said, 'Do you remember me? I am Joykrishna Mitter's son, Felu.'

Rajen Babu looked a little taken aback at first. Then his face broke into a smile. 'Felu? Of course I remember you. My word, you have become a young man! How is everyone at home? Is your father here?'

As Feluda answered these questions, I sat trying to hide my astonishment. How unfair the whole thing was—why hadn't Feluda told me that he knew Rajen Babu?

It turned out that Rajen Babu had worked in Calcutta for many years as a lawyer. He had once helped Feluda's father fight a case. He had come to Darjeeling and settled here ten years ago, soon after his retirement.

Feluda introduced me to him. He showed no sign of recognition. Perhaps the matter of offering me a lozenge a week ago had slipped his mind completely.

'You're fond of antiques, I see,' said Feluda conversationally.

'Yes. It's turned almost into an obsession.'

'How long—?'

'Over the last six months. But I've managed to collect quite a lot of things.'

Feluda cleared his throat. Then he told Rajen Babu what he had heard from me, and ended by saying, 'I still remember how you had helped my father. If I could do anything in return . . . *'

Rajen Babu looked both pleased and relieved. But before he could say anything, Tinkori Babu walked into the room. From the way he was breathing, it appeared that he had just come back after his evening walk. Rajen Babu made the introductions. 'Tinkori Babu happens to be a neighbour of Gyanesh, a friend of mine. When this friend heard that I was going to let one of my rooms, he suggested that I give it to Tinkori Babu. He would have gone to a hotel otherwise.'

Tinkori Babu laughed. 'I did hesitate to take up his offer, I must admit, chiefly because of my special weakness for cheroots. You see, Rajen Babu might well have objected to the smell. So I wrote to him first to let him know. He said he didn't mind, so here I am.'

'Are you here simply for a change of air?'

'Yes, but the air, I've noticed, isn't as cool and fresh as one might have expected.'

'Are you fond of music?' asked Feluda unexpectedly.

'Yes, but how did you guess?' Tinkori Babu gave a startled smile.

'Well, I noticed your finger,' Feluda explained. 'You were

tapping it on top of your walking stick, in keeping with the rhythm of that song from the radio.'

'You're quite right,' Rajen Babu laughed, 'he sings Shyamasangeet.'

Feluda changed the subject. 'Do you have the letter here?' he asked.

'Oh yes. Right next to my heart,' said Rajen Babu and took it out of the inside pocket of his jacket. Feluda spread it out.

It was not handwritten. A few printed words had been cut out of books or newspapers and pasted on a sheet of paper. 'Be prepared to pay for your sins,' it read.

'Did this come by post?'

'Yes. It was posted in Darjeeling, but I'm afraid I threw the envelope away.'

'Have you reason to suspect anyone?'

'No. For the life of me, I cannot recall ever having harmed anyone.'

'Do certain people visit you regularly?'

'Well, I don't get too many visitors. Dr Phoni Mitra comes occasionally if I happen to be ill.'

'Is he a good doctor?'

'About average, I should say. But then, my complaints have always been quite ordinary—I mean, no more than the usual coughs and colds. So I haven't had to look for a really good doctor.'

'Does he charge a fee?'

'Of course. But that's hardly a problem. I've got plenty of money, thank God.'

'Who else visits you?'

'A Mr Ghoshal has recently started coming to my house . . . look, here he is!' A man of medium height wearing a dark suit was shown into the room.

'Did I hear my name?' he asked with a smile.

'Yes, I was just about to tell these people that you share my interest in antiques. Allow me to introduce them.'

After exchanging greetings, Mr Ghoshal—whose full name was Abanimohan Ghoshal—said to Rajen Babu, 'I thought I'd drop by since you didn't come to the shop today.'

'N-no, I wasn't feeling very well, so I decided to stay in.'

It was clear that Rajen Babu did not want to tell Mr Ghoshal about the letter. Feluda had hidden it the minute Mr Ghoshal had walked in.

'All right, if you're busy today, I'll come back another time . . . actually, I wanted to take a look at that Tibetan bell,' said Mr Ghoshal.

'Oh, that's not a problem at all. I'll get it for you.' Rajen Babu disappeared into the house to fetch the bell.

'Do you live here in Darjeeling?' Feluda asked Mr Ghoshal, who had picked up a dagger and was looking at it closely. 'No,' he replied, turning the dagger in his hand. 'I don't stay in any one place for very long. I have to travel a lot. But I like collecting curios.' Feluda told me afterwards that a curio was a rare and ancient object of art.

Rajen Babu returned with the bell. It was really striking to look at. Its base was made of silver, the handle was a mixture of brass and copper, which was studded with colourful stones.

Mr Ghoshal took a long time to examine it carefully. Then he put it down on a table and said, 'You got yourself a very good deal there. It's absolutely genuine.'

'Ah, that's a relief. You're the expert, of course. The man at the shop told me it came straight out of the household of the Dalai Lama.'

'That may well be true. But I don't suppose you'd want to part with it? I mean . . . suppose you got a handsome offer?'

Rajen Babu shook his head, smiling sweetly.

'No. You see, I bought that bell simply because I liked it. I have no wish to sell it only to make money.'

'Very well,' Mr Ghoshal rose. 'I hope you'll be out and about tomorrow.'

'Thank you. I hope so, too.'

When Mr Ghoshal had gone, Feluda said to Rajen Babu, 'Don't you think it might be wise not to go out of the house for the next few days?'

'Yes, you're probably right. But this business of an anonymous letter is so incredible that I cannot really bring myself to take it seriously. It just seems like a foolish practical joke!'

'Well, why don't you stay in until we can be definite about that? How long have you had that Nepali servant?'

'Right from the start. He is completely reliable.'

Feluda now turned to Tinkori Babu. 'Do you stay at home most of the time?'

'Yes, but I go for morning and evening walks, so I'm out of the house for a couple of hours every day. In any case, should there be any real danger, I doubt if I could do anything to help. I am sixty-four, younger than Rajen Babu by only a year.'

'Don't involve poor Tinkori Babu in this, please,' Rajen Babu said. 'After all, he's come here to relax, so let him enjoy himself. I'll stay in if you insist, together with my servant. You two can come and visit me every day, if you so wish.'

'All right.'

Feluda stood up. So did I. It was time to go.

There was a fireplace in front of us. Over it, on a mantelshelf, were three framed photographs. Feluda moved closer to the fireplace to look at these. 'My wife,' said Rajen Babu, pointing at the first photograph. 'She died barely five years after our marriage.'

The second photo was of a young boy, who must have been about my own age when the photo was taken. A handsome boy indeed. 'Who is this?' Feluda asked.

Rajen Babu began laughing. 'That photo is there simply to show how time can change everything. Would you believe that that is my own photograph, taken when I was a child? I used to go to a missionary school in Bankura in those days. My father was the magistrate there. But don't let those angelic looks deceive you. I might have been a good-looking child, but I was extremely naughty. My teachers were all fed up with me. In fact, I didn't spare the students, either. I remember having tripped the best runner in our school in a hundred-yards race to stop him from winning.'

The third photo was of a young man in his late twenties.

It turned out to be Rajen Babu's only child, Prabeer Majumdar.

'Where is he now?' Feluda asked.

Rajen Babu cleared his throat. 'I don't know,' he said after a pause. 'He left home sixteen years ago. There is virtually no contact between us.'

Feluda started walking towards the front door. 'A very interesting case,' he muttered. Now he was talking like the detectives one reads about.

We came out of the house. It was already dark outside. Lights had been switched on in every house nestling in the hills. A mist was rising from the Rangeet valley down below. Rajen Babu and Tinkori Babu both walked up to the gate to see us off. Rajen Babu lowered his voice and said to Feluda, 'Actually, I have to confess that despite everything, I do feel faintly nervous. After all, something like this in this peaceful atmosphere was so totally unexpected . . . .'

'Don't worry,' said Feluda firmly. 'I'll definitely get to the bottom of this case.'

'Thank you. Goodbye!' said Rajen Babu and went back into the house. Tinkori Babu lingered. 'I am truly impressed by your power of observation,' he said. 'I, too, have read a large number of detective novels. Maybe I can help you with this case.'

'Really? How?'

'Look at the letter in your hand. Take the various printed words. Do they tell you anything?'

Feluda thought for a few seconds. 'The words were cut out with a blade, not scissors,' he said.

'Very good.'

'Second, each word has come from a different source—the typeface and the quality of paper vary from each other.'

'Yes. Can you guess what those different sources might be?'

'These two words—"prepared" and "pay"—appear to be a newspaper.'

'Right. *Ananda Bazar*.'

'How can you tell?'

'Only *Ananda Bazar* uses that typeface. And the other words were taken out of books, I think. Not very old books, mind you, for those different typefaces have been in use over the last twenty years, and no more. Apart from this, does the smell of the glue tell you anything?'

'I think the sender used Grippex glue.'

'Brilliant!'

'I might say the same for you.'

Tinkori Babu smiled. 'I try, but at your age, my dear fellow, I doubt if I knew what the word "detective" meant.'

We said namaskar after this and went on our way. 'I don't yet know whether I can solve this mystery,' said Feluda on the way back to our hotel, 'but getting to know Tinkori Babu would be an added bonus.'

'If he is so good at crime detection, why don't you let him do all the hard work? Why waste your own time making enquiries?'

'Ah well, Tinkori Babu might know a lot about printing and typefaces, but that doesn't necessarily mean he'd know everything!'

Feluda's answer pleased me. I bet Tinkori Babu isn't as clever as Feluda, I thought. Aloud, I said, 'Who do you suppose is the culprit?'

'The culp—' Feluda broke off. I saw him turn around and glance at a man who had come from the opposite direction and had just passed us.

'Did you see him?'

'No, I didn't see his face.'

'The light from that streetlamp fell on his face for only a second, and I thought—'

'What?'

'No, never mind. Let's go, I feel quite hungry.'

*

Feluda is my cousin. He and I were in Darjeeling with my father for a holiday. Father had got to know some of the other guests in our hotel fairly well, and was spending most of his time with them. He didn't stop us from going wherever we wished, nor did he ask too many questions.

I woke a little later than usual the next day. Father was in the room, but there was no sign of Feluda.

'Felu left early this morning,' Father explained. 'He said he'd try to catch a glimpse of Kanchenjunga.'

I knew this couldn't be true. Feluda must have gone out

to investigate, which was most annoying because he wasn't supposed to go out without me. Anyway, I had a quick cup of tea, and then I went out myself.

I spotted Feluda near a taxi stand. 'This is not fair!' I complained. 'Why did you go out alone?'

'I was feeling a bit feverish, so I went to see a doctor.'

'Dr Phoni Mitra?'

'Aha, you're beginning to use your brain, too!'

'What did he say?'

'He charged me four rupees and wrote out a prescription.'

'Is he a good doctor?'

'Do you think a good doctor would write a prescription for someone in perfect health? Besides, his house looked old and decrepit. I don't think he has a good practice.'

'Then he couldn't have sent that letter.'

'Why not?'

'A poor man wouldn't dare.'

'Yes, he would, if he was desperate for money.'

'But that letter said nothing about money.'

'There was no need to ask openly.'

'What do you mean?'

'How did Rajen Babu strike you yesterday?'

'He seemed a little frightened.'

'Fear can make anyone ill.'

'Oh?'

'Yes, seriously ill. And if that happened, he'd naturally turn to his doctor. What might happen then is something even a fathead like you can figure out, I'm sure.'

How clever Feluda was! But if Dr Mitra had really planned the whole thing the way Feluda described, he must be extraordinarily crafty, too.

By this time, we had reached the Mall. As we came near the fountain, Feluda suddenly said, 'I feel a bit curious about curios.' We were, in fact, standing quite close to the Nepal Curio Shop. Rajen Babu and Mr Ghoshal visited this shop every day. Feluda and I walked into the shop. Its owner came forward to greet us. He had a light grey jacket on, a muffler round his neck, and wore a black cap with golden embroidery. He beamed at us genially.

The shop was cluttered with old and ancient objects. A strange musty smell came from them. It was quiet inside. Feluda looked around for a while, then said, sounding important, 'Do you have good tankhas?'

'Come into the next room, sir. We've sold what was really good. But we're expecting some fresh stock soon.'

'What is a tankha?' I whispered.

'You'll know when you see one,' Feluda whispered back.

The next room was even smaller and darker. The owner of the shop brought out a painting of the Buddha, done on a piece of silk. 'This is the last piece left, but it's a little damaged,' he said. So this was a tankha! Rajen Babu had heaps of these in his house. Feluda examined the tankha like an expert, peering at it closely, and then looking at it from various angles. Three minutes later, he said, 'This doesn't appear to be more than seventy years old. I am looking for something much older than that, at least three hundred years, you see.'

'We're getting some new things this evening, sir. You might find what you're looking for if you came back later today.'

'This evening, did you say?'

'Yes, sir.'

'Oh, I must inform Rajen Babu.'

'Mr Majumdar? He knows about it already. All my regular customers are coming in the evening to look at the fresh arrivals.'

'Does Mr Ghoshal know?'

'Of course.'

'Who else is a regular buyer?'

'There's Mr Gilmour, the manager of a tea estate. He visits my shop twice a week. Then there's Mr Naulakha. But he's away in Sikkim at present.'

'All right, I'll try to drop in in the evening . . . Topshe, would you like a mask?' I couldn't resist the offer. Feluda selected one himself and paid for it. 'This was the most horrendous of them all,' he remarked, passing it to me. He had once told me there was no such word as 'horrendous'. It was really a mixture of 'tremendous' and 'horrible'. But I must say it was rather an appropriate word for the mask.

Feluda started to say something as we came out of the shop, but stopped abruptly. I found him staring at a man once again. Was it the same man he had seen last night? He was a man in his early forties, expensively dressed in a well-cut suit. He had stopped in the middle of the Mall to light his pipe. His eyes were hidden behind dark glasses. Somehow he looked vaguely familiar, but I couldn't recall ever having met him before.

Feluda stepped forward and approached him. 'Excuse me,' he said, 'are you Mr Chatterjee?'

'No,' replied the man, biting the end of his pipe, 'I am not.'

Feluda appeared to be completely taken aback. 'Strange! Aren't you staying at the Central Hotel?'

The man smiled a little contemptuously. 'No, I am at the Mount Everest; and I don't have a twin,' he said and strode off in the direction of Observatory Hill.

I noticed he was carrying a brown parcel, on which were printed the words 'Nepal Curio Shop'.

'Feluda!' I said softly. 'Do you think he bought a mask like mine?'

'Yes, he may well have done that. After all, those masks weren't all meant for your own exclusive use, were they? Anyway, let's go and have a cup of coffee.' We turned towards a coffee shop. 'Did you recognize that man?' asked Feluda.

'How could I,' I replied, 'when you yourself failed to recognize him?'

'Who said I had failed?'

'Of course you did! You got his name wrong, didn't you?'

'Why are you so stupid? I did that deliberately, just to get him to tell me where he was staying. Do you know what his real name is?'

'No. What is it?'

'Prabeer Majumdar.'

'Yes, yes, you're right! Rajen Babu's son, isn't he? We saw his photograph yesterday. No wonder he seemed familiar. But of course now he's a lot older.'

'Even so, there are a lot of similarities between father and son. But did you notice his clothes? His suit must have been from London, his tie from Paris and shoes from Italy. In short, there's no doubt that he's recently returned from abroad.'

'But does that mean Rajen Babu doesn't know his own son is in town?'

'Perhaps his son doesn't even know that his father lives here. We should try to find out more.'

The plot thickens, I told myself, going up on the open terrace of the coffee shop. I loved sitting here. One could get such a superb view of the town and the market from here.

Tinkori Babu was sitting at a corner table, drinking coffee. He waved at us, inviting us to join him.

'As a reward for your powerful observation and expertise in detection, I would like to treat you to two cups of hot chocolate. You wouldn't mind, I hope?' he said with a twinkle in his eye. My mouth began to water at the prospect of a cup of hot chocolate. Tinkori Babu called a waiter and placed his order. Then he took out a book from his jacket pocket and offered it to Feluda. 'This is for you. I had just one copy left. It's my latest book.'

Feluda stared at the cover. 'Your book? You mean . . . you write under the pseudonym Secret Agent?' Tinkori Babu's eyes drooped. He smiled slightly and nodded. Feluda grew more excited. 'But you're my favourite writer! I've read all your books. No other writer can write mystery stories the way you do.'

'Thank you, thank you. To tell you the truth, I had come to Darjeeling to chalk out a plot for my next novel. But I've now spent most of my time trying to sort out a real life mystery.'

'I do consider myself very fortunate. I had no idea I'd get to meet you like this!'

'The only sad thing is that I have to go back to Calcutta. I'm returning tomorrow. But I think I may be of some help to you before I leave.'

'I'm very pleased to hear that. By the way, we saw Rajen Babu's son today.'

'What!'

'Only ten minutes ago.'

'Are you sure? Did you see him properly?'

'Yes, I am almost a hundred per cent sure. All we need to do is check with the Mount Everest Hotel, and then there won't be any doubt left.'

Suddenly, Tinkori Babu sighed. 'Did Rajen Babu talk to you about his son?' he asked.

'No, not much.'

'I have heard quite a lot. Apparently, his son had fallen into bad company. He was caught stealing money from his father's cupboard. Rajen Babu told him to get out of his house. Prabeer did leave his home after that and disappeared without a trace. He was twenty-four at the time. A few years later, Rajen Babu began to regret what he'd done and tried to track his son down. But there was no sign of Prabeer anywhere. About ten years ago, a friend of Rajen Babu came and told him he'd spotted Prabeer somewhere in England. But that was all.'

'That means Rajen Babu doesn't know his son is here in Darjeeling.'

'I'm sure he doesn't. And I don't think he should be told. After all, he's already had one shock. Another one might . . . ' Tinkori Babu stopped. Then he looked straight at Feluda and shook his head. 'I think I am going mad. Really, I should give up writing mystery stories.'

Feluda laughed. 'You mean it's only just occurred to you that the letter might have been sent by Prabeer Majumdar himself?'

'Exactly. But . . . I don't know . . . ' Tinkori Babu broke off absent-mindedly.

The waiter came back and placed our hot chocolates before us. This seemed to cheer him up. 'How did you find Dr Phoni Mitra?' he asked.

'Good heavens, how do you know I went there?'

'I paid him a visit shortly after you left.'

'Did you see me coming out of his house?'

'No. I found a cigarette stub on his floor. I knew he didn't smoke, so I asked him if he'd already had a patient. He said yes, and from his description I could guess that it was you. However, I didn't know then that you smoked. Now, looking at your slightly yellowish fingertips, I can be totally sure.'

'You really are a most clever man. But tell me, did you suspect Dr Mitra as well?'

'Yes. He doesn't exactly inspire confidence, does he?'

'You're right. I'm surprised Rajen Babu consults him rather than anyone else.'

'There's a reason for it. Soon after he arrived in Darjeeling, Rajen Babu had suddenly turned religious. It was Dr Mitra who had found him a guru at that time. As followers of the same guru, they are now like brothers.'

'I see. But did Dr Mitra say anything useful? What did you talk about?'

'Oh, just this and that. I went there really to take a look at the books on his shelves. There weren't many. Those that I saw were all old.'

'Yes, I noticed it, too.'

'Mind you, he might well have got hold of different books from elsewhere, just to get the right printed words. But I'm pretty certain that is not the case. That man seemed far too lazy to go to such trouble.'

'Well, that takes care of Dr Mitra. What do you think of Mr Ghoshal?'

'I don't trust him either. He's a crook. He pretends to be interested in art and antiques, but I think what he really wants to do is sell to foreign buyers at a much higher price what he can buy relatively cheaply here.'

'But do you think he might have a motive in sending a threatening letter to Rajen Babu?'

'I haven't really thought about it.'

'I think I might have stumbled onto something.'

I looked at Feluda in surprise. His eyes were shining with excitement.

'What do you mean?'

'I learnt today,' Feluda said, lowering his voice, 'that the shop they both go to is going to get some fresh supplies this evening.'

Tinkori Babu perked up immediately. 'I see, I see!' he exclaimed. 'A letter like that would naturally frighten Rajen Babu into staying at home for a few days. In the meantime, Abani Ghoshal would go in and make a clean sweep.'

'Exactly.'

Tinkori Babu paid for the chocolate and rose. We went out together. My heart was beating fast. Abani Ghoshal, Prabeer Majumdar and Dr Phoni Mitra. As many as three suspects. Who was the real culprit?

Tinkori Babu went home. Feluda and I walked over to the Mount Everest Hotel. They confirmed that a man called Prabeer Majumdar had checked in five days ago.

*

We were supposed to visit Rajen Babu in the evening. But it began to rain so heavily at around 4 p.m. that we were forced to stay in. Feluda spent that whole evening scribbling in a notebook. I was dying to find out what he was writing, but didn't dare ask. In the end, I picked up the book Tinkori

Babu had given Feluda and began reading it. It was so thrilling that in a matter of minutes, all thoughts of Rajen Babu went out of my mind.

The rain stopped at 8 p.m. But by then it was very cold outside. Father, for once, stood firm and refused to allow us to go out.

Feluda shook me awake the next morning. 'Get up, Topshe. Quick!'

'What—what is it?' I sat up.

Feluda whispered into my ear, speaking through clenched teeth. 'Rajen Babu's Nepali servant was here a few moments ago. He said Rajen Babu wants to see us, and it's urgent. Do you want to come with me?'

'Of course!'

We got ready and were in Rajen Babu's house in less than twenty minutes. We found him lying in his bed, looking pale and haggard. Dr Mitra was by his side, feeling his pulse; and Tinkori Babu was standing before him, fanning him with a hand-held fan, despite the cold.

Dr Mitra released his hand as we came in. Rajen Babu spoke with some difficulty. 'Last night . . . after midnight . . . I woke suddenly and there it was . . . in this room . . . I saw a masked face!' Rajen Babu continued. 'I can't tell you . . . how I spent the night!'

'Has anything been stolen?'

'No. But I'm sure he bent over me . . . only to take the keys from under my pillow. Oh, it was horrible . . . horrible!'

'Take it easy,' said the doctor. 'I'm going to give you something to help you sleep. You need complete rest.' He stood up.

'Dr Mitra,' said Feluda suddenly, 'did you go to see a patient last night? Your jacket's got a streak of mud on it.'

'Oh yes,' Dr Mitra replied readily enough. 'I did have to go out last night. Since I have chosen to dedicate my life to my patients, I can hardly refuse to go out when I'm needed, come rain or shine.'

He collected his fee and left. Rajen Babu sat up in his bed. 'I feel a lot better now that you're here,' he admitted. 'I did feel considerably shaken, I must say. But now I think I might be able to go and sit in the living room.' Feluda and Tinkori Babu helped him to his feet. We made our way to the living room.

'I rang the railway station to change my ticket,' said Tinkori Babu. 'I don't want to leave today. But they said if I cancelled my ticket now, they couldn't give me a booking for another ten days. So I fear I've got to go.' This pleased me. I wanted Feluda to solve the mystery single-handedly.

'My servant was supposed to stay in yesterday,' Rajen Babu explained, 'but I myself told him to take some time off. His father is very ill, you see. He went home last night.'

'What did the mask look like?' Feluda asked.

'It was a perfectly ordinary mask, the kind you can get anywhere in Darjeeling. There are at least five of those in this room. There's one, look!' The mask he pointed out was almost an exact replica of the one Feluda had bought me yesterday.

Tinkori Babu spoke again. 'I think we ought to inform the police. We can no longer call this a joke. Rajen Babu may need protection. Felu Babu, you can continue with your investigation, nobody will object to that. But having thought things over, I do feel the police should know what's happened. I'll go myself to the police station right away. I don't think your life's in any danger, Rajen Babu, but please keep an eye on that Tibetan bell.'

We decided to take our leave. But before we left, Feluda said, 'Since Tinkori Babu is leaving today, you're going to be left with a vacant room, aren't you? Would you mind if we came and spent the night in it?'

'No, no, why should I mind? You're like a son to me. I'd be delighted. To tell you the truth, I'm beginning to lose my nerve. Those who are reckless in their youth generally tend to grow rather feeble in their old age. At least, that's what has happened to me.'

'I'll come and see you off at the station,' Feluda said to Tinkori Babu.

We passed the curio shop on our way back. Neither of us could help look inside. We saw two men looking around and talking. From the easy familiarity with which they were talking, it seemed as if they had known each other for a long time. One of them was Abani Ghoshal. The other was Prabeer Majumdar. I glanced at Feluda. He didn't seem surprised at all.

We went to the station at half-past ten to say goodbye to Tinkori Babu. He arrived in five minutes. 'My feet ache from having walked uphill,' he said. I noticed he was walking with a slight limp. 'Besides,' he added, 'it took me a while to buy this. I know Rajen Babu couldn't go to the curio shop but they really did get a lot of good stuff yesterday. So I chose something for him this morning. Will you please give it to him with my good wishes?'

'Certainly,' said Feluda, taking a brown packet from Tinkori Babu. 'There's one thing I meant to ask you. If I solve this mystery, I'd like to tell you about it. Will you give me your address, please?'

'You'll find the address of my publisher in my book. He'll forward all letters addressed to me. Goodbye . . . good luck!'

He climbed into a blue first-class carriage. The train left.

'That man would have made a lot of money and quite a name for himself if he had lived abroad. He has a real talent for writing crime stories,' Feluda remarked.

*

We returned to our hotel from the station. But Feluda went out again and, this time, refused to take me with him. When he finally came back, it was time to go to Rajen Babu's house to stay the night. As we set off, I said to him, 'You might at least tell me where you were during the day.'

'I went to various places. Twice to the Mount Everest

Hotel, once to Dr Mitra's house, then to the curio shop, the library and one or two other places.'

'I see.'

'Is there anything else you'd like to know?'

'Have you been able to figure out who is the real cul—?'

'The time hasn't come to disclose that. No, not yet.'

'But who do you suspect the most?'

'I suspect everybody, including you.'

'Me?'

'Yes. Anyone who has a mask is a suspect.'

'Really? In that case, why don't you include yourself in your list?'

'Don't talk rubbish.'

'I'm not! You didn't tell me that you knew Rajen Babu, which means you were not totally honest with me. Besides, you could have easily used that mask. I did not hide it anywhere, did I?'

'Shut up, shut up!'

Rajen Babu seemed a lot better when we arrived at his house, although he still looked faintly uneasy. 'I felt fine during the day,' he told us, 'but I must say I'm beginning to feel nervous again now it's getting dark.'

Feluda gave him the packet from Tinkori Babu. Rajen Babu opened it quickly and took out a beautiful statue of the Buddha, the sight of which actually moved him to tears.

'Did the police come to make enquiries?' asked Feluda.

'Oh yes. They asked a thousand questions. God knows if they'll get anywhere, but at least they've agreed to post someone outside the house during the night. That's a relief, anyway. In fact, if you wish to go back to your hotel, it will be quite all right.'

'No, we'd rather stay here, if you don't mind. It's too noisy in our hotel. I need peace and quiet to think about this case.'

Rajen Babu smiled. 'Of course you can stay. You'll get your peace and quiet here, and I can promise you an excellent meal. That Nepali boy is a very good cook. I've asked him to make his special chicken curry. The food in your hotel could never be half as tasty, I'm sure.'

We were shown to our room. Feluda stretched out on his bed and lit a cigarette. I saw him blow out five smoke rings in a row. His eyes were half-closed. After a few seconds of silence, he said, 'Dr Mitra did go out to see a patient last night. I found that out this morning. A rich businessman who lives in Card Road. He was with his patient from eleven-thirty to half-past twelve.'

'Does that rule him out completely?'

Feluda did not answer my question. Instead, he said, 'Prabeer Majumdar has lived abroad for so long and has such a lot of money that I can't see why he should suddenly arrive here and start threatening his father. He stands to gain very little, actually. Why, I learnt that he recently made a packet at the local races!'

I sat holding my breath. It was obvious that Feluda hadn't finished. I was right. Feluda stubbed out his cigarette and continued, 'Mr Gilmour has come to Darjeeling from his tea estate. I met him at the Planters' Club. He told me there was only one Tibetan bell that had come out of the palace of the Dalai Lama, and it is with him. The one Rajen Babu has is a fake. Abani Ghoshal is aware of it.'

'You mean the bell that we saw here isn't all that valuable?'

'No. Besides, both Abani Ghoshal and Prabeer Majumdar were at a party last night, from 9 p.m. to 3 a.m. They got totally drunk, I believe.'

'That man wearing a mask came here soon after midnight, didn't he?'

'Yes.'

I began to feel rather strange. 'Well then, who does that leave us with?'

Feluda did not reply. He sighed and rose to his feet. 'I'm going to sit in the living room for a minute,' he said. 'Do not disturb me.'

I took his place on the bed when he left. It was getting dark, but I felt too lazy to get up and switch on the lights. Through the open window I could see lights in the distance, on Observatory Hill. The noise from the Mall had died down. I heard the sound of hooves after a while. They got louder and louder, then slowly faded away.

It soon grew almost totally dark. The hill and the houses on it were now practically invisible. Perhaps a mist was rising again. I began to feel sleepy. Just as my eyes started to close, I suddenly sensed the presence of someone else in the room. My blood froze. Too terrified to look in the direction of the door, I kept my eyes fixed on the window. But I could feel the man move closer to the bed. There, he was now standing right next to me, and was leaning over my face. Transfixed, I watched his face come closer . . . oh, how horrible it was . . . a mask! He was wearing a mask!

I opened my mouth to scream, but an unseen hand pulled the mask away, and my scream became a nervous gasp. 'Feluda! Oh my God, it's you!'

'Had you dozed off? Of course it's me. Who did you think . . .?' Feluda started to laugh, but suddenly grew grave. Then he sat down next to me, and said, 'I was simply trying on all those masks in the living room. Why don't you wear this one for a second?' He passed me his mask. I put it on.

'Can you sense something unusual?'

'Why, no! It's a size too large for me, that's all.'

'Think carefully. Isn't there anything else that might strike you as odd?'

'Well . . . there's a faint smell, I think.'

'Of what?'

'Cheroot?'

'Exactly.'

Feluda took the mask off. My heart started to beat faster again.

'T-t-t-inkori Babu?' I stammered.

Feluda sighed. 'Yes, I'm afraid so. It must have been extremely easy for him. He had access to all kinds of printed material; and you must have noticed he was limping this morning. That might have been the result of jumping out of a window last night. But what I totally fail to understand is his motive. He appeared to respect Rajen Babu a lot. Why then did he do something like this? What for? Perhaps we shall never know.'

*

The night passed peacefully and without any further excitement. In the morning, just as we sat down to have breakfast with our host, his Nepali servant came in with a letter for him. It was once again a blue envelope with a Darjeeling post-mark.

Rajen Babu went white. He took out the letter with a trembling hand and passed it to Feluda. 'You read it,' he said in a low voice.

Feluda read it aloud. This is what it said:

Dear Raju,

When I first wrote to you from Calcutta after Gyanesh told me you had a house in Darjeeling, I had no idea who you really were. But that photograph of yours on your mantelshelf told me instantly that you were none other than the boy who had once been my classmate in the missionary school in Bankura fifty years ago.

I did not know that the desire for revenge would raise its head even after so many years. You see, I was the boy you tripped at that hundred-yards race on our sports day. Not only did I miss out on winning a medal and setting a new record, but you also managed to injure me pretty seriously. Unfortunately, my father got transferred to a different town only a few days after this incident, which was why I never got the chance to have a showdown with you then; nor did you ever learn just how badly you had hurt me, both mentally and physically. I had to spend three months in a hospital with my leg in a cast.

When I saw you here in Darjeeling, leading such a comfortable and peaceful life, I suddenly thought of doing something that would cause you a great deal of anxiety and ruin your peace of mind, at least for a short time. This was my way of settling scores, and punishing you for your past sins.

With good wishes,

Yours sincerely,

Tinu

(Tinkori Mukhopadhyaya)

Translated by Gopa Majumdar

Kailash Chowdhury's Jewel

'See how you like my card.'

Feluda fished out a visiting card from his wallet and held it before me. It said: Pradosh C. Mitter, Private Investigator. Feluda was clearly trying to publicize what he did for a living. And why not? After his success over the missing diamond ring that had once belonged to Emperor Aurangzeb, he was fully entitled to tell everyone how clever he had been. But, of course, he didn't really have to worry about publicity. A lot of people had come to know about the case, anyway. In fact, Feluda had received a couple of offers already, but he didn't accept them as they were not challenging enough.

He put the card back in his wallet, and stretched his legs

on the low table in front of him. 'It looks like I shall get the chance to exercise my brain during this Christmas break,' he said casually.

'Why? Have you found a new mystery?' I asked. Feluda's words had made me quite excited, but I didn't show it. He took out a small box from a side pocket and helped himself to some supari from it. 'You appear greatly excited,' he observed.

What? How did he guess? Feluda explained even before I could ask. 'Are you wondering how I knew? It isn't always possible to hide your feelings, you know, even if you try. Little things often give one away. When I made that remark about working during this Christmas break, you were about to yawn. My words made you close your mouth abruptly. If you were truly indifferent to what I said, you'd have finished your yawn in the usual way, without breaking it off.'

Once again I was startled by his powers of observation. 'Without being able to observe and take in even the minutest detail, no one can claim to be a detective,' Feluda had often said to me. 'Sherlock Holmes has shown us the way. All we need to do is follow him.'

'You didn't tell me why you will need to exercise your brain,' I reminded him.

'Have you heard of Kailash Chowdhury, of Shyampukur?'

'No. There are so many famous people in our city. I cannot have heard of all of them. I am only fifteen!'

Feluda lit a cigarette. 'His family owned a lot of land in Rajshahi. They were zamindars. But they also had property in Calcutta, so they moved here after Partition. Kailash Chowdhury is a lawyer. He used to go on shikar and, in fact, became quite well-known as a shikari. He even wrote two books on the subject. Sometime ago, an elephant went mad in the Jaldapara Reserve Forest and began creating such havoc that Kailash Babu was called in to kill it. His name was mentioned in almost every paper.'

'I see. What has all this to do with your brain? Is there a mystery regarding Kailash Chowdhury?'

Instead of giving me an answer, Feluda took out a letter from the front pocket of his jacket and passed it to me. 'Read it,' he said. I unfolded the letter and read what it said:

Dear Mr Mitter,

I decided to write to you after seeing your advertisement in the *Amrita Bazar Patrika*. I should be much obliged if you could come and meet me at the above address. I am sending this letter by express delivery. It should, therefore, reach you tomorrow. I shall expect you the day after, i.e. on Saturday, at 10 a.m.

Yours sincerely,
Kailash Chowdhury.

'But it's Saturday today!' I exclaimed, 'and nine o'clock already!'

'You're improving every day. I am very glad to note that you remember days and dates so well.'

A sudden doubt raised its head in my mind. 'This letter speaks only of meeting you. What if he objects to an extra person?'

Feluda took the letter back from me, and folded it carefully before replacing it in his pocket.

'He might not, as you're a young boy. He might not see you as sufficiently important to object to. But if he does, we'll pack you off to another room. You can wait there while we finish our talk.'

My heart began beating faster. I had been wondering what to do in the Christmas holidays. Now it seemed as if I was in for a very interesting time.

We got off a tram near Shyampukur Street at five minutes to ten. Feluda had stopped on the way to buy a book written by Kailash Chowdhury. It was called *The Passion of Shikar*. He leafed through it in the tram, and said, as we got down, 'God knows why a brave man like him needs to see a private detective!'

Kailash Chowdhury's house, 51 Shyampukur Street, turned out to be a huge old mansion. A long drive led to the main house. There were gardens on both sides, marble statues and a fountain. We passed these and made our way to the front door. There were footsteps on the other side within thirty seconds of pressing the bell. One look at the man who opened the door told me it was not Kailash Chowdhury. No brave shikari could have such a mouse-like appearance. He was a man of medium height, rather plump, possibly no more than thirty years old. His eyes held a look of childlike innocence. In his hand was a magnifying glass.

'Whom would you like to see?' he asked. His voice was as mild as his appearance.

Feluda took out one of his cards and handed it to the gentleman. 'I have an appointment with Mr Chowdhury. He asked me to come here.'

The man cast a quick glance at the card, and said, 'Please come in.'

We followed him down the hall, up a flight of stairs and were ushered into what looked like a small office.

'Please have a seat. I'll go and inform my uncle,' he said and disappeared.

We took two old chairs with arms that faced an equally old table, painted black. Three sides of the room were lined with glass cases filled with books. On the table I noticed something interesting. Three fat stamp albums were stacked one on top of the other, and a fourth was lying open. Rows of stamps had been carefully pasted in it. A few loose stamps lay in a cellophane packet, together with the usual paraphernalia of stamp collectors: hinges, a pair of tweezers and a stamp catalogue. Now it was clear why the man who met us at the door was carrying a magnifying glass. He was obviously the collector of these stamps.

Feluda, too, was looking at these objects, but before either of us could make a remark, the same man returned and said, 'Uncle asked you to wait in the drawing room. He'll join you shortly.'

We were taken to the drawing room. It was a large room, with a chandelier, oil paintings, marble statues and a great number of vases that were strewn all over. Everything in it bore the mark of life during the Raj, at least life in an affluent household. On the floor was the skin of a Royal Bengal tiger, and from the walls stared four heads of deer, two cheetahs and a wild buffalo.

Nearly ten minutes later, a middle-aged man entered the room. He seemed pretty strong and agile for his age. His features were sharp, and he sported a thin moustache. He was wearing a red silk dressing gown over a pyjama-kurta.

We rose to our feet and said, 'Namaskar.' Mr Chowdhury returned our greeting, but raised his eyebrows slightly on seeing me.

'This is my cousin,' Feluda explained. Mr Chowdhury took the smaller sofa next to ours, and asked, 'Do you carry out your investigations together?'

Feluda laughed, 'No, not really. But Tapesh happened to be involved in all the cases I have handled so far. He's never caused any trouble.'

'Very well. Abanish, you may go now; and see if you can arrange a cup of tea for these people.'

The stamp-collector was standing near the door. At these words, he disappeared inside. Kailash Chowdhury looked at Feluda, and said, 'I hope you don't mind, but I'd like to see the letter I wrote to you. Did you bring it?'

Feluda smiled. 'Is this to make sure I am the right person? Here's your letter, sir.'

Mr Chowdhury glanced briefly at the letter, said 'Thank you', and returned it to Feluda.

'One has to be careful in these matters, I'm sure you understand. Anyway, I assume you know a little bit about my work. I am known as a shikari.'

'Yes, sir. I did know that.'

Mr Chowdhury pointed at the heads of various animals on the walls and said, 'I killed all those. I learnt to use a rifle at the age of seventeen. Before that, as a child, I had used air guns and killed small birds. I am not afraid to fight anyone— or anything—if I can face my opponent, if I can see him. But if the adversary is a secret one . . . if he doesn't come out in the open . . . what does one do?'

He paused. I could feel my heart thudding faster again. The details of a mystery were about to be revealed, but Mr Chowdhury was beating about the bush so much that the suspense was getting higher every minute. A few seconds later, he resumed speaking. 'I didn't expect you to be so young,' he said. 'How old are you?'

'Twenty-eight.'

'I see. Well, I could have gone to the police. But I don't really have a lot of faith in them. Instead of helping, they usually make a total nuisance of themselves. Besides, I respect the young. So you may well be the right person for the job. I think an old head on young shoulders can achieve a lot more than an entire police force.'

He paused again. Feluda seized this opportunity to ask quickly, 'If you could tell me what the problem is . . .?'

Silently, Mr Chowdhury took out a piece of paper from his pocket and passed it to Feluda. 'See what you can make of it,' he said. Feluda unfolded it. I leant across and read what was written on it:

Do not make things worse for yourself. You must return what does not belong to you. Go to Victoria Memorial on Monday, and leave it under the first plant of the first row of lilies that faces the south gate. This must be done by 4 p.m. Do not try to inform the police, or go to a detective. If you do, you will end up exactly like the animals you killed on your shikar.

'What do you think?' Mr Chowdhury asked gravely.

Feluda stared at the note for a few moments. Then he said, 'The writer tried to mask his handwriting, for the same letters have been written in different ways. And he wrote on the top sheet of a new pad.'

'How can you tell?'

'If you write on a pad, the leaves below the top one always carry a faint impression of what is written on the upper sheet. It may not be legible, but it is there. This sheet is absolutely smooth.'

'Very good. Can you tell anything else?'

'No, it's impossible to say anything more simply by looking at it. Did this arrive by post?'

'Yes. The postmark said Park Street Post Office. I got this note three days ago. Today is Saturday, the 20th.'

Feluda returned the note to Mr Chowdhury and said, 'I would now like to ask you a few questions, if I may. You see, I know nothing about your life, except the tales of shikar that you wrote.'

'Very well. Go ahead with your questions. But please help yourself to the sweets before you begin.'

A bearer had come in a few minutes earlier and placed a silver plate before us, loaded with sweets. Feluda did not have to be told a second time. He picked up a rasgulla and popped it into his mouth. 'What,' he asked after a while, 'is this object that doesn't belong to you?'

'Frankly, Mr Mitter, I cannot think of anything like that at all. Everything I possess in this world, including things in this house, were either inherited or bought by me. Everything . . . except . . .' he stopped abruptly.

'Except what?'

'Well, there is something that's both valuable and tempting.'

'What is it?'

'A stone.'

'A precious stone?'

'Yes.'

'Did you buy it?'

'No.'

'Did it belong to your forefathers?'

'No, I found it in a jungle in Madhya Pradesh. There were four of us. We chased a tiger into the jungle and finally killed it. Then we found this ancient and abandoned temple. The stone was fixed on the forehead of the statue of the deity. I don't think anyone even knew of its existence.'

'Were you the first to see it?'

'Everyone else saw the temple, but yes, I was the first to notice the stone.'

'Who else was with you?'

'An American called Wright, a Punjabi called Kishorilal and my brother, Kedar.'

'Is your brother also a shikari?'

'He used to go on shikar with me sometimes, but now I don't know what he does. He went abroad four years ago.'

'Abroad?'

'Switzerland. Something to do with making watches.'

'When you found the stone, what happened? Didn't any of the others want to take it?'

'No, because none of us realized its value then. I came to know only when I had it assessed by a jeweller in Calcutta.'

'Who else got to know?'

'Not many people. I haven't got many relations. A couple of friends know about it, I told Kedar, and I think my nephew Abanish is aware of its value.'

'Do you keep the stone here in your house?'

'Yes, in my bedroom.'

'Why don't you keep it in a bank locker?'

'I did once. The very next day, I was almost run over by a car. Oh, I had a narrow escape, I can tell you. That made me think if I was separated from the stone it would bring me bad luck. Yes, I know it's superstition. Nevertheless, I brought it back from the bank.'

Feluda had finished eating. I could tell from the way he was frowning that he had started to think. He wiped his mouth, drank some water and said, 'Who else lives in this house?'

'My nephew, Abanish, and three old servants. Then there's my father, but he's very old and almost totally senile. One of the servants spends all his time looking after him.'

'What does your nephew do?'

'Nothing much, really. His passion is philately. He's talking of starting a shop to sell stamps.'

Feluda was quiet for a few moments, as if he was trying to come to a decision about something. Then he said slowly, 'Would you like me to find out who wrote that note?'

Mr Chowdhury seemed to force a smile. 'I am getting old, Mr Mitter. I can do without anxiety and tension. And it isn't just that note. Last night this man rang me. I couldn't recognize his voice. He said if I didn't place that object at the specified time and place, he'd come into my house and cause me bodily harm. But even so, I am not willing to part with that stone. Besides, this man cannot possibly have a legitimate claim on it. He's just hoping to frighten me by his threats. A crook like him ought to be punished. You must work out how.'

'There is only one thing that I can possibly do. I must go to Victoria Memorial on Monday and keep an eye on the lilies. This man has got to turn up.'

'He may not come himself.'

'That shouldn't matter. If we can catch whoever comes hoping to collect the stone, it won't be difficult to find out who is really behind the scene.'

'But the man might be dangerous. When he turns up at Victoria Memorial and discovers I have not placed the stone under that plant, God knows what he might do. Can't you do anything to find out who he is before Monday? I mean, there's that note and the phone call. Isn't that enough?'

Feluda got up and began pacing. 'Look, Mr Chowdhury,' he said, 'this man has said you'd get into trouble if you went to a private detective. Now, whether or not I take any action, you might be in trouble already. So really, you must decide whether you want me to go ahead.' Mr Chowdhury wiped his face with a handkerchief, although it was quite cold inside the room. 'You, and this young cousin of yours . . . well, you don't appear to be investigators. This is an advantage. I mean, people may have heard your name, but how many know what you look like? No, I don't think there's much chance of you being recognized as the detective I have hired. If you are still prepared to take this job, I will certainly pay you your fee.'

'Thank you. But before I go, I would like to see that stone.'

'Sure.'

All of us got up. The stone was kept in the wardrobe in his bedroom, Mr Chowdhury said. We followed him upstairs. A marble staircase went up to the first floor, ending at one end of a long, dark corridor. There were rooms on either side of the corridor. I did not actually count them, but at a guess there were at least ten rooms. Some of them were locked. There was no one in sight. The slightest noise sounded unnaturally loud in the eerie silence. I began to feel uneasy.

Mr Chowdhury's bedroom was the last one on the right. When we were more or less half way down the corridor, I suddenly realized that the door to one of the rooms was ajar. Through a small gap, a very old man was peering out, craning his neck to look at us. His eyes were dimmed with age, but as we got closer, I was shocked to notice the expression in them. The old man was staring with murder in his eyes. But he said nothing. I now felt positively scared.

'That's my father,' Mr Chowdhury explained hurriedly, continuing to walk, 'I told you he was senile, didn't I? He keeps peeping out of doors and windows. And he thinks everyone neglects him. That's why he looks so cross most of the time. But I can assure you every effort is made to make sure he's all right.'

The bedroom had a huge, high bed, and the wardrobe was next to it. Mr Chowdhury opened it, pulled out a drawer and took out a small, blue velvet box from it. 'I bought this box from a jeweller just to keep the stone in it,' he informed us, and opened it. A glittering stone lay inside, about the size of a litchi, radiating a greenish-blue light.

'This is a blue beryl. It's usually found in Brazil. There cannot be many of these in India, and certainly none of this size. I know that for a fact.'

Feluda picked up the stone, held it between his forefinger

and thumb and looked closely at it for a few moments before returning it to its owner. Mr Chowdhury put it back in the drawer, then took out his wallet from his pocket. 'This is an advance payment,' he said, offering five crisp ten-rupee notes, 'I'll pay you the rest when this business is cleared up. All right?'

'Thank you,' said Feluda, accepting the money. This was the first time I saw him actually being paid for his services.

'I will need that note you were sent, and I'd like to speak to your nephew, please,' Feluda said, as we climbed down the stairs. The phone in the drawing room started ringing just as we reached the last step. Mr Chowdhury went quickly to answer it, leaving us behind. 'Hello!' we heard him say. This was followed by silence.

When we entered the drawing room a few seconds later, Mr Chowdhury replaced the receiver and sat down quickly, looking pale and frightened. 'It . . . it was that same voice!' he whispered.

'What did it say?'

'It simply repeated the same threat, but this time it was more specific. He actually said he wanted what I had found in an abandoned temple.'

'Did he say anything else?'

'No.'

'And you didn't recognize the voice?'

'No, all I can say is that it was a most unpleasant voice. Maybe you'd like to think again about taking on this case?'

Feluda smiled. 'I have finished thinking,' he replied.

We left the drawing room soon after this and made our way to the room of Mr Chowdhury's nephew, Abanish Babu. We found him closely examining something on a table with a magnifying glass. As we entered the room, he swiftly covered the object with one hand and got to his feet.

'Come in, come in!' he invited.

'I can see that you are very interested in stamps,' Feluda remarked. Abanish Babu's eyes lit up. 'Yes, sir. That's my only interest in life, my only passion. All I ever think of are stamps!'

'Do you specialize in any one country, or do you collect stamps from all over the world?'

'I used to collect them from wherever they happened to be, but of late I've started to concentrate on India. I had to sift through hundreds of old letters to get them.'

'Did you find anything good?'

'Good? Good?' Abanish Babu began to look ecstatic, 'Are you interested in this subject? Will you understand if I explain?'

'Try me,' Feluda smiled, 'I don't claim to be an expert, but like most other people, I was once keen on collecting stamps, and dreamt of acquiring the famous ones. You know, the one-penny stamp from the Cape of Good Hope, the two-penny from Mauritius and the 1856 ones from British Guiana. Ten years ago their price was in the region of a hundred thousand rupees. Now they must be worth a lot more.'

Abanish Babu grew even more excited. 'Well then,' he said

with gleaming eyes, 'Well then, I'm sure you'd understand. I'd like to show you something. Here it is.' He took his hand off the table and revealed the object he had been hiding. It turned out to be very old stamp, detached from an envelope. Its original colour must have been green, but it had faded almost completely. Abanish Babu passed it to Feluda.

'What? What can you see?' he asked eagerly.

'An Indian stamp, about a hundred years old. It has a picture of Queen Victoria. I've seen such stamps before.'

'Have you? Yes, I'm sure you have. Now then, take another look through this magnifying glass.'

Feluda peered through the proffered glass.

'Now what do you see, eh?' Abanish Babu asked anxiously.

'There is a printing error.'

'Exactly!'

'The word is obviously POSTAGE, but instead of a 'G', they printed a 'C'.'

Abanish Babu took the stamp back. 'Do you know how much that stamp is worth because of that error?'

'How much?'

'Twenty thousand.'

'What!'

'Yes, sir. I've checked with the authorities in UK. The catalogue does not mention the error. I was the first person to find it.'

'Congratulations! But . . . er . . . I wanted to discuss something else with you, Abanish Babu. I mean, something other than stamps.'

'Yes?'

'Your uncle—Kailash Chowdhury—has a valuable jewel. Are you aware of that?'

Abanish Babu had to think for a few moments before replying, 'Oh yes, yes. I did hear about it. I know nothing about its value, but it's supposed to be "lucky", or so my uncle said. Please forgive me, Mr Mitter, but of late I have been able to pay no attention to anything except my stamps.'

'How long have you lived in this house?'

'For the last five years. I moved here soon after my father died.'

'Do you get on with your uncle?'

'Which one do you mean? I have two uncles. One of them lives abroad.'

'Oh? I was speaking of Kailash Babu.'

'I see. Well, he is a very nice man, but . . . '

'But what?'

Abanish Babu frowned. 'For the last few days . . . he's been sort of . . . different.'

'How do you mean? When did you first notice this?'

'Two or three days ago. I told him about this stamp, but he paid no attention at all. Normally, he takes a great deal of interest. Besides, some of his old habits seem to be changing.'

'How?'

'He used to take a walk in the garden every morning before breakfast. He hasn't done that for the last couple of days. In fact, he gets up quite late. Maybe he hasn't been sleeping well.'

'Do you have any particular reason to say this?'

'Yes. My bedroom is on the ground floor. The room directly above mine is my uncle's. I have heard him pacing in the middle of the night. I've even heard his voice. I think he was having an argument.'

'An argument? With whom?'

'Probably grandfather. Who else could it be? I've even heard footsteps going up and coming down the stairs. One night, I got up and went to the bottom of the stairs to see what was going on. I saw my uncle coming down from the roof, with a gun in his hand.'

'What time would that have been?'

'Around two o'clock in the morning, I should think.'

'What's there on the roof?'

'Nothing except a small attic. It was full of old papers and letters, but I took those away a month ago.'

Feluda rose. I could see he had no further questions to ask.

Abanish Babu said, 'Why did you ask me all this?'

Feluda smiled. 'You uncle has a lot on his mind at this moment. But you don't have to worry about it. Once things get sorted out, I'll come and have a look at your stamps. All right?'

We returned to the drawing room to say goodbye to Mr Chowdhury.

'I cannot guarantee anything, obviously, but I would like to say one thing,' Feluda told him, 'Please stop worrying and leave everything to me. Try to sleep at night. Take a sleeping pill, if necessary; and please do not go up to the roof. The houses in your lane are so close to one another that, for all we know, your enemy might be hiding on the roof of the house next door to keep an eye on you. If that is the case, he may well jump across and attack you.'

'You think so? I did go up to the roof one night, but I took my gun with me. I'd heard a strange noise, you see. But I couldn't see anyone.'

'I hope you always keep your gun handy?'

'Oh yes. But mental tension and anxiety can often affect one's aim. If this business isn't cleared up soon, God knows what's going to happen to mine.'

*

The next day was Sunday. Feluda spent most of his time pacing in his room. At around four, I saw him change from his comfortable kurta-pyjama into trousers and a shirt.

'Are you going out?' I asked.

'Yes. I thought it might be a good idea to take a look at the lilies in the Victoria Memorial. You can come with me, if you like.'

We took a tram and got off at the crossing of Lower Circular Road. Then we walked slowly to the south gate of the memorial. Not many people came here. In the evening, particularly, most people went to the front of the building, to the north gate.

We slipped in through the gate. Twenty yards to the left,

there stood rows of lilies. The blue beryl was supposed to be kept the next day under the first row of these. The sight of these flowers—beautiful though it was—suddenly gave me the creeps.

'Didn't your father have a pair of binoculars, which he'd taken to Darjeeling?' Feluda asked.

'Yes, he's still got them.'

'Good.'

We spent about fifteen minutes walking in the open ground surrounding the building. Then we took a taxi to the Lighthouse cinema. I got out with Feluda, feeling quite puzzled. Why did he suddenly want to see a film? But no, he was actually interested in a bookshop opposite the cinema. After leafing through a couple of other books, he picked up a fat stamp catalogue and began thumbing through its pages. I peered over his shoulder and whispered, 'Are you suspecting Abanish Babu?'

'Well, if he's so passionately fond of stamps, I'm sure he wouldn't mind laying his hands on some ready cash.'

'But . . . remember that phone call that came when we were still at Mr Chowdhury's? Abanish Babu could not have made it, surely?'

'No. That was made by Akbar Badshah. Or it may have been Queen Victoria.'

This made me realize Feluda was no longer in the right mood to give straight answers to my questions, so I shut up.

It was eight o'clock by the time we got back home. Feluda took off his jacket and threw it on his bed. 'Look up Kailash

Chowdhury's telephone number in the directory while I have a quick shower,' he said.

I sat down with the directory in my lap, but the phone started ringing before I could turn a single page. Considerably startled, I picked it up.

'Hello.'

'Who is speaking?'

What a strange voice! I had certainly never heard it before.

'Who would you like to speak to?' I asked. The answer came in the same harsh voice: 'Why does a young boy like you go around with a detective? Don't you fear for your life?'

I tried calling out to Feluda, but could not speak. My hands had started to tremble. Before I could replace the receiver, the man finished what he had to say, 'I am warning you—both of you. Lay off. Or the consequences will be . . . unhappy.'

I sat still in my chair, quite unable to move. Feluda walked into the room a few minutes later, and said, 'Hey, what's the matter? Why are you sitting in that corner so quietly? Who rang just now?'

I swallowed hard and told him what had happened. His face grew grave. Then he slapped my shoulder and said, 'Don't worry. The police have been informed. A few men in plain clothes will be there. We must be at Victoria Memorial tomorrow.'

I didn't find it easy to sleep that night. It wasn't just the telephone call that kept me awake. I kept thinking of Mr

Chowdhury's house and all that I had seen in it: the staircase with the iron railing that went right up to the roof; the long, dark veranda with the marble floor on the first floor, and the old Mr Chowdhury peering out of a half-open door. Why was he staring at his son like that? And why had Kailash Babu gone to the roof carrying his gun? What kind of noise had he heard?

Feluda said only one thing before switching off his light, 'Did you know, Topshe, that people who send anonymous notes and threaten others on the telephone are basically cowards?' It was perhaps because of this remark that I finally fell asleep.

*

Feluda rang Kailash Chowdhury the following morning and told him to relax and stay at home. Feluda himself would take care of everything.

'When will you go to Victoria Memorial?' I asked him.

'The same time as yesterday. By the way, do you have a sketch pad and pens and other drawing material?'

I felt totally taken aback. 'Why? What do I need those for?'

'Never mind. Have you got them or not?'

'Yes, of course. I have my school drawing book.'

'Good. Take it with you. I'd want you to stand at a little distance from the lilies, and draw something—the trees, the building, the flowers, anything. I shall be your drawing teacher.'

Feluda could draw very well. In fact, I knew he could draw a reasonable portrait of a man after seeing him only once. The role of a drawing teacher would suit him perfectly.

Since the days were short in winter, we reached the Victoria Memorial a few minutes before four o'clock. There were even fewer people around today. Three Nepali ayahs were roaming idly with their charges in perambulators. An Indian family—possibly Marwaris—and a couple of old men were strolling about, but there was no one else in sight. At some distance away from the gate, closer to the compound wall, stood two men under a tree. Feluda glanced at them, and then nudged me quietly. That meant those two were his friends from the police. They were in plain clothes, but were probably armed. Feluda knew quite a lot of people in the police.

I parked myself opposite the rows of lilies and began sketching, although I could hardly concentrate on what I was doing. Feluda moved around with a pair of binoculars in his hands, occasionally grabbing my pad to make corrections and scolding me for making mistakes. Then he would move away again, and peer through the binoculars.

The sun was about to set. The clock in a church nearby struck five. It would soon get cold. The Marwaris left in a big car. The ayahs, too, began to push their perambulators towards the gate. The traffic on Lower Circular Road had intensified. I could hear frequent horns from cars and buses, caught in the evening rush. Feluda returned to me and was about to sit down on the grass, when something near the gate seemed to attract his attention. I followed his gaze quickly, but could see no one except a man wrapped in a brown shawl, who was standing by the road outside, quite a long way away from the gate. Feluda placed the binoculars to his eyes, had a quick look, then passed them to me. 'Take a look,' he whispered.

'You mean that man over there? The one wearing a shawl?'

'Hm.'

One glance through the binoculars brought the man clearly into view, as if he was standing only a few feet away. I gave an involuntary gasp. 'Why . . . this is Kailash Chowdhury himself!'

'Right. Perhaps he's come to look for us. Let's go.'

But the man began walking away just as we started to move. He was gone by the time we came out of the gate. 'Let's go to his house,' Feluda suggested, 'I don't think he saw us. He must have gone back feeling worried.'

There was no chance of finding a taxi at this hour, so we began walking towards Chowringhee in the hope of catching a tram. The road was heavily lined with cars. Soon, we found ourselves outside the Calcutta Club. What happened here was so unexpected and frightening that even as I write about it, I can feel myself break into a cold sweat. I was walking by Feluda's side when, without the slightest warning, he pulled me sharply away from the road. Then he leapt aside himself, as a speeding car missed him by inches.

'What the devil—!' Feluda exclaimed. 'I missed the number of that car.'

It was too late to do anything about that. Heaven knew where the car had come from, or what had possessed its driver to drive so fast in this traffic. But it had disappeared totally from sight. I had fallen on the pavement, my sketch pad and pencils had scattered in different directions. I picked myself up, without bothering to look for them. If Feluda hadn't seen that car coming and acted promptly, there was no doubt that both of us would have been crushed under its wheels.

Feluda did not utter a single word in the tram. He just sat looking grim. The first thing he said on reaching Mr Chowdhury's house was: 'Didn't you see us?'

Mr Chowdhury was sitting in a sofa in the drawing room. He seemed quite taken aback by our sudden arrival. 'See you?' he faltered, 'Where? What are you talking about?'

'You mean to say you didn't go to Victoria Memorial?'

'Who, me? Good heavens, no! I didn't leave the house at all. In fact, I spent all afternoon in my bedroom upstairs, feeling sick with worry. I've only just come down.'

'Well then, Mr Chowdhury, do you have an identical twin?'

Mr Chowdhury's jaw fell open. 'Oh God, didn't I tell you the other day?'

'Tell me what?'

'About Kedar? He's my twin.'

Feluda sat down quickly. Mr Chowdhury's face seemed to have lost all colour.

'Why, did you . . . did you see Kedar? Was he there?' he asked anxiously.

'Yes. It couldn't possibly have been anyone else.'

'My God!'

'Why do you say that? Does your twin have a claim on that stone?'

Mr Chowdhury suddenly went limp, as though all the energy in his body had been drained out. He leant against the arm of his sofa, and sighed. 'Yes,' he said slowly, 'yes, he does. You see, it was Kedar who found the stone first. I saw the temple, but Kedar was the one who noticed the stone fixed on the statue.'

'What happened next?'

'Well, I took it from him. I mean, I pestered and badgered him until he got fed up and gave it to me. In a way, it was the right thing to do, for Kedar would simply have sold it and wasted the money. When I learnt just how valuable the stone was, I did not tell Kedar. To be honest, when he left the country, I felt quite relieved. But now . . . perhaps he's come back because he couldn't find work abroad. Maybe he wants to sell the stone and start a business of his own.'

Feluda was silent for a few moments. Then he said, 'Do you have any idea what he might do next?'

'No. But I do know this: he will come and meet me here. I have stopped going out of the house, and I did not keep the stone where I was told to. There is no other way left for him now. If he wants the stone, he has to come here.'

'Would you like me to stay here? I might be able to help.'

'No, thank you. That will not be necessary. I have now made up my mind, Mr Mitter. If Kedar wants the stone, he can have it. I will simply hand it over to him. It's simply a matter of waiting until he turns up. You have already done so much, putting your life at risk. I am most grateful to you. If you send me your bill, I will let you have a cheque.'

'Thank you. You're right about the risk. We nearly got run over by a car.'

I had realized a while ago that one of my elbows was rather badly grazed, but had been trying to keep it out of sight. As we rose to take our leave, Feluda's eyes fell on it. 'Hey, you're hurt, aren't you?' he exclaimed, 'Your elbow is bleeding! If you don't mind, Mr Chowdhury, I think Tapesh should put some Dettol on the wound, or it might get septic. Do you—?'

'Yes, yes,' Mr Chowdhury got up quickly, 'You are quite right. The streets are filthy, aren't they? Wait, let me ask Abanish.'

We followed Mr Chowdhury to Abanish Babu's room. 'Do we have any Dettol in the house, Abanish?' Mr Chowdhury asked. Abanish Babu gave him a startled glance.

'Why, I saw you bring a new bottle only a week ago!' he said. 'Don't tell me it's finished already?'

Mr Chowdhury gave an embarrassed laugh. 'Yes, of course. I totally forgot. I am going mad.'

Five minutes later, my elbow duly dabbed with Dettol, we came out of the house. Instead of going towards the main road where we might have caught a tram to go home, Feluda began walking in the opposite direction. Before I could ask him anything, he said, 'My friend Ganapati lives nearby. He promised to get me a ticket for the Test match. I'd like to see him.'

Ganapati Chatterjee's house turned out to be only two houses away. I had heard of him, but had never met him before. He opened the door when Feluda knocked: a rather plump man, wearing a pullover and trousers.

'Felu! What brings you here, my friend?'

'Surely you can guess?'

'Oh, I see. You needn't have come personally to remind me. I hadn't forgotten. I did promise, didn't I?'

'Yes, I know. But that's not the only reason why I am here. I believe there's a wonderful view of north Calcutta from your roof. I'd like to see it, if you don't mind. Someone I know in a film company told me to look around. They're making a film on Calcutta.'

'Okay, no problem. That staircase over there goes right up to the roof. I'll see about getting us a cup of tea.'

The house had four storeys. We got to the top and discovered that there was a very good view of Mr Chowdhury's house on the right. The whole house—from the garden to the roof—was visible. A light was on in one of the rooms on the first floor, and a man was moving about in it. It was Kailash Chowdhury's father. I could also see the attic on the roof. At least, I could see its window; its door was probably on the other side, hidden from view

Another light on the second floor was switched on. It was the light on the staircase. Feluda took out the binoculars again and placed them before his eyes. A man was climbing the stairs. Who was it? Kailash Chowdhury. I could recognize his red silk dressing gown even from this distance. He disappeared from view for a few seconds, then suddenly appeared on the roof of his house. Feluda and I ducked promptly, and hid behind the wall that surrounded Ganapati Chatterjee's roof, peering cautiously over its edge.

Mr Chowdhury glanced around a couple of times, then went to the other side of the attic, presumably to go into it through the door we could not see. A second later, the light in the attic came on. Mr Chowdhury was now standing near its window with his back to us. My heart began beating faster. Mr Chowdhury stood still for a few moments, then bent down, possibly sitting on the ground. A little later, he stood up, switched the light off and went down the stairs once more.

Feluda put the binoculars away and said only one thing: 'Fishy. Very fishy.'

*

He didn't speak to me on our way back. When he gets into one of these moods, I don't like to disturb him. Normally, if he is agitated about something, he starts pacing in his room. Today, however, I saw him throw himself down on his bed and stare at the ceiling. At half past nine, he got up and started to scribble in his blue notebook. I knew he was writing in English, using Greek letters. So there was no way I could read and understand what he'd written. The only thing that was obvious was that he was still working on Mr Chowdhury's case, although his client had dispensed with his services.

I lay awake for a long time, which was probably why I didn't wake the following morning until Feluda shook me. 'Topshe! Get up quickly, we must to go Shyampukur at once.'

'Why?' I sat up.

'I rang the house, but no one answered. Something is obviously wrong.'

In ten minutes, we were in a taxi, speeding up to Shyampukur Street. Feluda refused to tell me anything more, except, 'What a cunning man he is! If only I'd guessed it a little sooner, this would not have happened!'

When we reached Mr Chowdhury's house, Feluda saw that the front door was open and walked right in, without bothering to ring the bell. We crossed the landing and arrived at Abanish Babu's room. The sight that met my eyes made me gasp in horrified amazement. A chair lay overturned before a table, and next to it, lay Abanish Babu. His hands were tied behind his back, a large handkerchief covered his mouth. Feluda bent over him quickly and untied him.

'Oh, oh, thank God! Thank you!' he exclaimed, breathing heavily.

'Who did this to you?'

'Who do you think?' he sat up, still panting. 'My uncle—Kailash Mama did this. I told you he was going crazy, didn't I? I got up quite early this morning, and decided to get some work done. It was still dark outside, so I switched the light on. My uncle walked in soon after that. The first thing he did was switch the light off. Then he struck my head, and I fell immediately. Everything went dark. I regained consciousness a few minutes before you arrived, but could neither move nor speak. Oh God!' he winced.

'And Kailash Babu? Where is he?' Feluda shouted.

'No idea.'

Feluda turned and leapt out of the room. I followed a second later.

There was no one in the drawing room. We lost no time in going upstairs, taking three steps at a time. Kailash Chowdhury's bedroom was empty, although the bed looked as though it had been slept in. The wardrobe had been left open. Feluda pulled a drawer out and found the small blue velvet box. When he opened it, I was somewhat surprised to see that the blue beryl was still in it, quite intact.

By this time, Abanish Babu had arrived at the door, still looking pathetic. 'Who has the key to the attic?' Feluda demanded. Abanish Babu seemed taken aback by the question.

'Th-that's with my uncle!' he said.

'Okay, let's go up there,' Feluda announced, grabbing Abanish Babu by his shoulders and dragging him up the dark staircase.

We reached the roof, only to find that the attic was locked. A padlock hung at the door. Anyone else would have been daunted by the sight. But Feluda stepped back, then ran forward and struck the door with his shoulder, using all his strength. On his third attempt, the door gave in noisily. A few old rusted nails also came off the wall. Even I was surprised by Feluda's physical strength.

The room inside was dark. We stepped in cautiously. A few seconds later, when my eyes got used to the dark, I noticed another figure lying in one corner, bound and gagged exactly like Abanish Babu. Who was this? Kailash Chowdhury? Or was it Kedar?

Without a word, Feluda released him from his bondage and then carried him down to the bedroom. The man spoke only when he had been placed comfortably in his bed.

'Are you . . . the . . . ?' he asked feebly, staring at Feluda.

'Yes, sir. I am Pradosh Mitter, the detective. I suppose it was you who had written me that letter, but of course I never got the chance to meet you. Abanish Babu, could you get him some warm milk, please?'

I stared at the man in amazement. So this was the real Kailash Chowdhury! He propped himself up on a pillow and said, 'I was physically strong, so I managed to survive somehow. Otherwise . . . in these four days . . . '

Feluda interrupted him, 'Sh-sh. You mustn't strain yourself.'

'No, but I have to tell you a few things. Or you'll never get the whole picture. There was no way I could meet you personally, you see, for he captured me the day I wrote to you. He dropped something in my tea, which made me virtually unconscious. He could never have overpowered me in any other way.'

'And he began to pass himself off as Kailash Chowdhury from that day?'

Kailash Babu nodded his head sadly. 'It is my own fault, Mr Mitter. I cannot blame anyone else. Our entire family suffers from one big weakness. We are all given to exaggerating the simplest things, and telling tall stories for no reason at all. I had bought that stone in Jabalpore for fifty rupees. I have no idea what possessed me to tell Kedar a strange story about a temple in a jungle, and a statue with that stone fixed on its forehead. He swallowed the whole thing, and began to eye that stone from that day. He envied me for many reasons. Perhaps he could not see why I should be so lucky, so successful in life, when he appeared to fail in everything he did. After all, we were identical twins, our fortunes should not have been so very different. Kedar had always been the black sheep—reckless and unscrupulous. Once he got mixed up with a gang that made counterfeit money. He would have gone to jail, but I managed to save him.

'Then he went abroad, after borrowing a great deal of money from me. I was glad. Good riddance, I thought. But only about a week ago, I came back home one day and found the stone missing. I never imagined for a moment that Kedar had come back and stolen it from my room. I rounded up all the servants and shouted at them, but nothing happened. Two days later, I wrote to you. Kedar turned up the same evening, and returned the stone to me. He was absolutely livid, for by this time, he had learnt that it had no value at all. He had been dreaming of getting at least a hundred thousand for it. He said he needed money desperately, would I give him twenty thousand? I refused. So he waited till I ordered a cup of tea, then managed to drug me and carry me up to the attic. When I woke, he told me he'd keep me there until I agreed to do as told. In the meantime, he'd pretend to be me, and he'd tell my office I was on sick leave.'

'He obviously did not know you had written to me,' Feluda added, 'So when we turned up, he took ten minutes to write a fake anonymous note and then gave us a cock-and-bull story about an imaginary enemy. If he didn't, he knew I'd get suspicious. At the same time, my presence in this house or in his life was highly undesirable. So he tried a threat on the telephone, then got in a car and tried to run us over.'

Kailash Chowdhury frowned. 'That makes perfect sense,' he said. 'What doesn't, is why he left so suddenly. I did not agree to give him a single paisa. So why did he leave? Surely he didn't leave empty-handed?'

'No, no, no!' shouted a voice at the door. None of us had seen Abanish Babu return with a glass of milk. 'Why should he leave empty-handed?' he screamed. 'He took my stamp! That precious, rare Victorian stamp has gone.'

Feluda stared at him, wide-eyed. 'What! He took your stamp?'

'Yes, yes. Kedar Mama has ruined me!'

'How much did you say it was worth?'

'Twenty thousand.'

'But—' Feluda turned to Abanish Babu and lowered his

voice, 'according to the catalogue, Abanish Babu, it cannot possibly fetch more than fifty rupees.'

Abanish Babu went visibly pale.

'The Chowdhurys are prone to exaggerate everything to make an impression,' Feluda continued, 'and you are their nephew. So presumably, you inherited the same trait. Am I right?'

Abanish Babu began to look like a child who had lost his favourite toy. 'What was I supposed to do?' he said with a tragic air, 'I spent three years going through four thousand stamped envelopes. Not one of them was any good, except that one. Oh, all right, it wasn't much, but people believed my story. I got them interested!'

Feluda started laughing. 'Never mind, Abanish Babu,' he said, thumping his back, 'I think your uncle is going to be suitably punished, and that should give you some comfort. Let me ring the airport. You see, I had guessed he might try to escape this morning. So I rang Indian Airlines, and they told me he had a booking on their morning flight to Bombay. I began to suspect your uncle only when he said he couldn't remember having bought a new bottle of Dettol just a few days ago.'

*

The police had no problem in arresting Kedar Chowdhury; and Abanish Babu's stamp was duly returned to him. Feluda was paid so handsomely by Kailash Babu that, even after eating out three times, and seeing a couple of films with me, he still had a substantial amount left in his wallet.

Today, as we sat having tea at home, I said to him, 'Feluda, I have been thinking this through, and have reached a conclusion. Will you please tell me if I am right?'

'Okay. What have you been thinking?'

'It's about Kailash Chowdhury's father. I think he knew what Kedar had done. I mean, maybe a father can tell the difference between identical twins. Perhaps that's the reason why he was throwing such murderous glances at his son.'

'That may or may not be the case. But since your thoughts appear to be the same as mine on this subject, I am hereby rewarding you for your intelligence.'

So saying, Feluda coolly helped himself to a jalebi from my plate.

Translated by Gopa Majumdar

Gopa Majumdar has translated several works from Bengali to English, the most notable of these being Ashapurna Debi's Subarnalata *and Bibhutibhushan Bandopadhyay's* Aparajito, *for which she won the Sahitya Akademi Award in 2001. She has translated several volumes of Satyajit Ray's short stories and all of the Feluda stories for Penguin Books India.*

One Dozen Stories

With Puffin Classics, the story isn't over
when you reach the final page.
Want to discover more about
the author and his world?
Read on . . .

CONTENTS

NAME: Satyajit Ray

BORN: 2 May 1921 in a progressive Brahmo family of Kolkata

FATHER: Famous writer, poet and printing technologist Sukumar Ray

MOTHER: Suprabha Ray

QUALIFICATIONS: BA in Economics (Hons) from Presidency College, Kolkata. Trained in Oriental Art for three years at Vishwa Bharati University (founded by Rabindranath Tagore).

PROFESSIONAL LIFE: Worked in advertising agency DJ Keymer for almost twelve years. Started as a Junior Visualizer and went on to become Art Director.

MARRIED TO: Bijoya Ray

CHILDREN: One son, Sandip Ray, also a film-maker.

FAMOUS FOR: Internationally acclaimed films. One of the earliest Indian directors to have won prizes at major film festivals around the world like Cannes, Venice, Berlin, London, San Francisco, etc. An extremely versatile person, he wrote the script, composed the music, designed the sets and costumes, prepared posters in addition to directing the films.

Ray was also a writer of repute, and his short stories, novellas, poems and articles, written in Bengali, have been immensely popular. He wrote several books in Bengali, most of which became bestsellers. He also illustrated his own books.

MAJOR AWARDS: Bharat Ratna, highest civilian award of India; Legion D'Honneur, highest civilian award of France; Oscar for Lifetime Achievement.

What is the Twelve Stories series?

Apart from the stories about detective Feluda and Professor

Shonku the scientist, Satyajit Ray wrote 101 short stories. Most of them were for children and were first published in children's magazines like *Sandesh* and *Anandamela*. Subsequently, they were printed as collections of twelve stories. This book is a translation of the first collection *Ek Dojon Goppo* (One Dozen Stories). The second collection is *Aro Ek Dojon* (One More Dozen).

After this, the titles of the collections were interesting wordplays on the Bengali word for twelve (*baro*): *Aro Baro* (Twelve More), *Ebaro Baro* (Twelve Again), *Bah! Baro* (Wow! Twelve) and *Jobor Baro* (Solid Twelve) were names of subsequent collections.

Another book in the series was *Eker Pithey Dui* (Two On One). This title was taken from a poem by Ray's father Sukumar Ray. (A translation of the full poem is available in the book *Wordygurdyboom! The Nonsense World of Sukumar Ray*, also published by Puffin India in the Puffin Classics series.)

Who was Feluda?

Satyajit Ray's most famous creation, detective Feluda, made his debut in a tale of straightforward detection, set in Darjeeling. This is described in the story 'Danger In Darjeeling' in this collection. He is a cousin of the narrator (Tapesh Ranjan Mitra a.k.a Topshe). On his debut, he was nothing but a twenty-seven-year-old intelligent young man with a job, in Darjeeling on vacation. In fact, the tone of Feluda in this short story is a little childish and his adversary is a strong character (Tinkori Babu). It was only during his second adventure in Lucknow, 'The Emperor's Ring' (*Badshahi Angti*), that Feluda became a hero. But even in Lucknow, he is an amateur detective who has a full-time job and solves mysteries as a hobby.

From his third story onwards ('Kailash Chowdhury's Jewel', also included in this collection), Feluda started to take detection seriously and became a professional detective. The visiting card he got printed spelt out his name and occupation: Pradosh C. Mitter, Private Investigator. He appeared in thirty-five stories and novels, all of which went on to become hot favourites with millions of fans.

Were these stories ever made into films?

Each of Ray's short stories have a tight plot and end with a nice twist in the tale. When his son Sandip Ray made the television serial *Satyajit Ray Presents* he took most of the stories from his father's works. The serial was made in two parts. In the first part, there were thirteen short stories—one per episode—and was televised in 1985. A second part had two long stories and a Feluda novella, all based on Ray's writings. Ray himself made movies out of two Feluda stories—*Shonar Kella* (The Golden Fortress) and *Joi Baba Felunath* (The Elephant God).

Satyajit Ray Presents was similar in nature and style to the famous American series of the 1950s and 1960s, *Alfred Hitchcock Presents*. These were half-hour episodes of mystery, suspense, crime and drama which were typical of the Hitchcock style of storytelling. The show was voted by *Time* magazine as one of 'The 100 Best TV Shows of All Time'. Alfred Hitchcock—maker of suspense masterpieces like *Psycho* and *Rebecca*—also did not direct the series and only introduced it in a humorous style. He once said, 'The television is bringing back murder to its rightful setting – the living room.'

Indian cities and towns in Satyajit Ray's works

A hallmark of Ray's stories and novels is the accuracy in the description of the settings. Interestingly, almost all the settings were places where he had shot his films. Since shooting a film required extensive knowledge of the terrain, he used these details when he created the backdrop for his stories.

He shot in rural West Bengal for several of his films like *Pather Panchali* (1955), *Abhijan* (1962) and *Goopy Gyne Bagha Byne* (1968). Of course, the city of Kolkata, where he lived and worked, featured prominently in his works. Many Feluda stories are set in unusual locations within the city, for e.g,, the Park Street cemetery in *Gorosthaney Shabdhan* (*The Secret of the Cemetery*, Puffin India, 2004).

Darjeeling—the setting for the first Feluda story and one more later on—was where he also shot his first colour film, *Kanchenjangha* (1962). For orderly shooting and movement, Satyajit Ray drew up an extremely accurate map of the hill station, which is quite amazing, since he used no equipment to do so.

Nicknames

Most Bengali people have a nickname, which could be a shorter version of his formal name or it could be completely different altogether. Satyajit Ray's nickname was Manik, literally meaning 'jewel'. To his cast, crew and lots of fans, he was Manikda.

Pradosh C. Mitter's nickname is Felu, which doesn't really mean

anything. His cousin Tapesh Ranjan is Topshe.

From the stories you have just read, can you fill up the following chart of nicknames and formal names?

Formal Name	Nickname
Sitalakanto Roy	
	Shibu
Tinkori Mukhopadhyay	

Satyajit Ray's stories cut across several genres and cover a wide variety of topics. The twelve stories in this collection are about very different things. Here is a list of the topics, a piece of trivia and something to think about each.

1. Carnivorous Plants
   Trivia: A vamp from the Batman series—Poison Ivy—maintains a garden of carnivorous and poisonous plants to kill her enemies.
   Where on earth are the most carnivorous plants found?

2. Aliens
   Trivia: Satyajit Ray wrote a script for a film called *The Alien* in 1967, which was an extended version of this short story. But it was never made into a film.
   Aliens—both good and bad—have appeared very often in movies. How many can you name? (Hint: Think Bollywood and Hollywood.)

3. Ghosts
   Trivia: A lot of people believe ghosts can be summoned and communicated with. They do this in a séance.
   Which is your favourite ghost story? Have you ever tried to write one?

4. Time Travel
   Trivia: H.G. Wells coined the term 'time machine' in a novel of the same name (published in 1895). The time machine was a device to travel back and forth in time.

If you had a time machine, where would you like to go—to the distant past or the alluring future?

5. Monsters
    Trivia: In the mythology of every culture, monsters are present in some form. In Hindu mythology, monsters are called rakshasas.
    Do you think Janardan Babu was really a monster? Or did Shibu imagine things?

6. Bats
    Trivia: The fear of bats is called Chiroptophobia.
    What is the fear of ghosts called?

7. Memory Lapse
    Trivia: Amnesia is the medical term for loss of memory.
    Have you seen any film in which a person loses his memory?

8. Magic
    Trivia: The magic trick involving the coin, ring and matchsticks was actually witnessed by Satyajit Ray at a wedding.
    How do you think the magician did this magic trick?

9. Film Shooting
    Trivia: Being an excellent artist, Ray often sketched the looks of the junior artistes he wanted for his films and bystanders at the location used to hunt for people who matched the sketch.
    Three kinds of moustache are mentioned in the story—walrus,

butterfly and Ronald Colman. Can you draw a picture of each?

10. Indigo
    Trivia: Right after the Revolt of 1857, indigo farmers also rose in protest against the brutal British planters and over the next decade, indigo cultivation was wiped out in India. *What was indigo used for? Why do you think Indian farmers were forced to cultivate it?*

11. Detection
    Trivia: The most famous detective in the world is Sherlock Holmes, created by Arthur Conan Doyle. A museum has been created at 221B Baker Street, London, where Holmes supposedly lived.
    Have you heard of a detective called Hercule Poirot? What was his nationality?

12. Stamp collecting
    Trivia: The 1856 one-cent 'Black on Magenta' stamp of British Guiana is regarded as the rarest stamp in the world. It is a rectangular stamp of black ink printed on magenta paper. It's corners are snipped off, so it actually has an octagonal shape.
    What is philately? Who coined the word?